M

Beaton, M. C. H

A Highland
Christmas.

$16.95   NOV   1999

DATE			
YOU ARE RESPONSIBLE FOR ANY DAMAGE AT TIME OF RETURN.			
4/14	44c	50cop	12/13
12/11	40	57	7/10
5/09	38c	55 cop	4/09
9/04	22c	35 cop	6/04
3/02	18c	60cop	3/02

A HIGHLAND CHRISTMAS

The Hamish Macbeth Mysteries

M.C. BEATON

A HIGHLAND CHRISTMAS

THE MYSTERIOUS PRESS

Published by Warner Books

A Time Warner Company

This book is a work of fiction. Names, characters, places, and incidents are the product of the author's imagination or are used fictitiously. Any resemblance to actual events, locales, or persons, living or dead, is co-incidental.

 Mysterious Press books are published by Warner Books, Inc., 1271 Avenue of the Americas, New York, NY 10020.

Visit our Web site at www.twbookmark.com

 A Time Warner Company

The Mysterious Press name and logo are registered trademarks of Warner Books, Inc.

Printed in the United States of America

First Printing: November 1999

10 9 8 7 6 5 4 3 2 1

Library of Congress Cataloging-in-Publication Data

Beaton, M. C.
    A Highland Christmas / M.C. Beaton.
        p.   cm.
    ISBN 0-89296-699-8
    I. Title.
PR6052.E196H54   1999
823'.914—dc21   99-14588
                                                 CIP

Book design and composition by L&G McRee

For Brian and Judith Harris
and their son, Adam
With love

A HIGHLAND CHRISTMAS

Chapter One

*M*ore and more people each year are going abroad for Christmas. To celebrate the season of goodwill towards men, British Airways slams an extra one hundred and four pounds on each air ticket. But the airports are still jammed.

For so many people are fleeing Christmas.

Fed up with the fact that commercial Christmas starts in October. Fed up with carols. Dreading the arrival of Christmas cards from people they have forgotten to send a card to. Unable to bear yet another family get-together with Auntie Mary puking up in the corner after sampling too much of the punch. You see at the airports the triumphant glitter in the eyes of people who are leaving it all behind, including the hundredth rerun of *Miracle on 34th Street.*

But in Lochdubh, in Sutherland, in the very far north of Scotland, there is nothing to flee from. Christmas, thought Hamish Macbeth gloomily, as he walked along the waterfront, his shoulders hunched against a tearing wind, was not coming to Lochdubh this year any more than it had come the previous years.

There was a strong Calvinist element in Lochdubh which frowned on Christmas. Christmas had nothing to do with the birth of Christ, they said, but was really the old Roman Saturnalia which the early Christians had taken over. And as for Santa Claus—forget it.

So there were no Christmas lights, no tree, nothing to sparkle in the dark winter.

P. C. Hamish Macbeth was feeling particularly sour, for his family had taken off for Florida for a winter vacation. His mother had won a family holiday for thinking up a slogan for a new soap powder—"Whiter Than The Mountain Snow"—and Hamish could not go with them. Sergeant Macgregor over at Cnothan was ill in hospital with a grumbling appendix and Hamish had been instructed to take over the sergeant's beat as well as do his own.

Hamish's family were unusual in that they had always celebrated Christmas — tree, turkey, presents and all. In parts of the Highlands, like Lochdubh, the old spirit of John Knox still wandered, blasting anyone with hellfire should they dare to celebrate this heathen festival.

Hamish had often pointed out that none other than Luther was credited with the idea of the Christmas tree, having been struck by the sight of stars shining through the branches of an evergreen. But to no avail. Lochdubh lay silent and dark beside the black waters of the loch.

He turned back towards the police station. The wind was becoming even more ferocious. The wind of Sutherland can sound frightening as it moves up from ordinary tumult to a high-pitched screech and then a deep booming roar.

Hamish decided to settle down with a glass of whisky in front of the television. He was just reaching up for the whisky bottle in one of the kitchen cupboards when he realized he had not checked the answering machine. He went through to the police office. There was one message, and it was Mrs. Gallagher saying she wanted him to call on her immediately as she wished to report a burglary.

Hamish groaned. "This is all I need," he said to the dingy, uncaring walls of the police office. He loathed Mrs. Gallagher. She was a tough, wiry old lady who ran her small croft single-handed. She lived out on the Cnothan road and was generally detested. She was described as crabbit, meaning "sourpuss." Mrs. Gallagher never had a good word to say for anybody. She had a genius for sniffing out the vulnerable points in anyone's character and going in for the kill.

In the far north of Scotland in winter, there are only a few hours of daylight. Hamish glanced at his watch. "Three o'clock and black as hell already," he muttered.

The wind cut like a knife as he climbed into the police Land Rover. As he held the wheel tightly against the buffeting of the wind and drove along the curving road out of the village, he realized that he had never questioned Mrs. Gallagher's bitterness. It had simply been one of those unpleasant facts of his existence since he had started policing in Lochdubh.

At last he bumped up the rutted track leading to the low croft house where Mrs. Gallagher lived. Bending his head against the ferocity of the wind, he rapped at the door. He waited as he heard her fumbling with locks and bolts. What was she afraid of? Most crofters didn't bother locking their doors.

Then he saw the gleam of an eye through the door, which she opened on a chain. She had always had all those locks. How on earth could anyone manage to get in and burgle her?

"Police," he said.

The chain dropped and the door opened wide. "Come ben," she said curtly.

He ducked his head and followed her in.

As in most croft houses, the kitchen was used as a living room with the parlour being kept for "best." That meant the parlour was usually only used for weddings and funerals. Mrs. Gallagher's kitchen was cosy and cheerful, belying the permanently sour expression on her face. She had a mass of thick crinkly pepper-and-salt hair. The skin of her face was like old leather, beaten into a permanent tan by working outdoors. Her eyes were that peculiar light grey, almost silver, you still see in the Highlands. Emotions flitted over the surface of such eyes like cloud shadows on the sea and yet rarely gave anything away.

"What's been taken?" asked Hamish.

"Sit down and stop looming over me," she snapped. Hamish obediently sat down. "My cat, Smoky's been stolen." Hamish had started to tug out his notebook, then left it alone.

"How long's the cat been gone?"

"Twenty-four hours."

"Look here, Mrs. Gallagher, it's probably strayed, gone wild or been killed by the fox." Like "the devil," it was always "the fox" in the Highlands of Scotland, where crofters had no sentimentality about an animal they damned as the worst piece of vermin in the country-side.

"Havers!" said Mrs. Gallagher. "If I say it is stolen, then it is stolen and it is your duty to get it back."

"I'll have a look around for it," said Hamish, struggling to rise out of the low chair on which he was sitting. "Is there any sign of a break-in? Any doors, locks or windows been tampered with?"

"Not a sign. But they could be too cunning for the likes of you. I want you to get a SOCO team out here," said Mrs. Gallagher. Hamish, who watched police soaps as well, knew she meant a Scene of Crime Operatives team. "Smoky was here with me. He didn't go out."

"Did you go out yourself?"

"Yes, I went to feed the sheep."

"And wouldn't Smoky nip out after you?"

"No, Smoky never goes out until dinner-time." Hamish interpreted "dinnertime" to mean midday. In most houses in and around Lochdubh, dinner was still in the middle of the day and high tea, that is, one course followed

by bread and scones and cakes and washed down with tea, in the early evening.

"I cannot order a forensic team frae Strathbane for a missing cat," said Hamish. "Anyway, they chust wouldn't come."

"Your trouble," said Mrs. Gallagher, "is that you are lazy. That is why you are still unmarried. You are too damn lazy to get off your scrawny backside to even court a lassie."

Hamish stood up and looked down at her. "I will look around outside for your cat and post a notice at the police station," he said evenly. "That iss all I can do." His Highland accent became more sibilant when he was angry or distressed.

"You have not even checked the doors or windows to see where they might have got in!" shouted Mrs. Gallagher. "I'll report you."

"Do that." Hamish put on his cap and let himself out.

The wind had died as suddenly as it had sprung up. It was still blowing hard far up in the sky, for ragged black clouds were tearing across a small cold moon. He set off over the surrounding fields calling "Smoky!" but there was no sign of any cat.

He wearily returned to the croft house and knocked on the door. Again he waited and called out "Police" in answer to her sharp demand to know who was there. "Have you got a photo of the cat?" he called. After some time, the door opened on the chain. She handed a photograph to him. "I want a receipt," she said. He wrote out a receipt and went on his way.

The next day, Hamish forgot about the cat. He had a more important burglary to investigate in a neighboring village.

Cnothan, less rigid on the subject of Christmas than Lochdubh, had planned to decorate its main street with fairy lights. Now they were gone. He set out, enjoying the faint glow from a red sun which shone low on the hills. All was still after the gales of the day before. Smoke rose up from cottage chimneys in straight lines. The waters of the sea loch were flat and still, one great mirror reflecting the clouds and mountains above.

Hamish did not like Cnothan, the least friendly place in the Highlands. He marvelled that Cnothan of all places should want to brighten the place up with lights. He went to the home of the chairman of the parish council, a Mr. Sinclair, who had reported the burglary. The door was opened by Mrs. Sinclair who told him he would find her husband at his shop in the main street. The shop, it turned out, sold electrical goods. Hamish grinned. Nothing like

Highland enterprise when it came to making money.

Mr. Sinclair was a smooth, pompous man. There is not much of a pecking order in the north of Scotland and so often the shopkeeper is head of the social world. He had an unlined olive face, despite his age which Hamish judged to be around fifty. His unnaturally black hair was combed straight back and oiled.

"Was the shop burgled?" asked Hamish, looking around.

"No, we didnae have the lights here," said Mr. Sinclair. "They were kept in a shed up by the community hall."

"Maybe you'd better take me there."

"You'll need to wait until I'm closed for lunch. This is my busiest season."

Hamish looked around the empty shop. "Doesn't look busy now."

"Temporary lull. Temporary lull."

Hamish looked at his watch. Ten to one. Oh, well, only ten minutes to wait. Sod's law, he thought bitterly as a woman came in at exactly two minutes to one and started asking about washing machines.

It was quarter past one before she finished asking questions and left without buying anything. "I hate that sort of woman," grumbled Mr. Sinclair after he had locked up and led the way up the main street at a brisk trot. "I think they come in just to pass the time. Here we are."

The door of the shed was open. A smashed padlock lay on the ground. "Did they take anything other than the lights?" asked Hamish.

"Yes," said Mr. Sinclair. "They took the big Christmas tree as well."

"Och, man, someone must hae seen someone carrying a great big tree!"

"You can ask. I've asked. Has anyone seen a thing? No."

Hamish squatted down and studied the ground. "There's no dragging marks," he said. "Must have been more than one o' them. How big was the tree?"

"About eight feet."

"Aye, well, one man would ha' dragged it. So it was several of them. And no one saw them. So it stands to reason they must have gone up the back way." He stood up and looked down at Mr. Sinclair from his greater height. "I never heard afore that the folks of Cnothan wanted anything to do with Christmas."

"I was elected chairman of the council this year and I managed to persuade them. I was backed by the minister. We took up a collection."

"And your shop supplied the lights?"

"Yes. Do you mind if I get home for something to eat?"

"You run along. I'll let you know if I find out anything."

Behind the community hall, Hamish noticed common grazing land. There was a gate leading into it. Hamish bent down again. There were little bits of fir needles on the ground. So they had gone this way. Where to? Who would want to take a Christmas tree and lights?

After searching around some more, he went into a cafe and ordered a sausage roll and a cup of coffee. The roll was greasy and the coffee, weak. He approached the slattern who ran the cafe and asked, "Are there folks in Cnothan who were against having Christmas lights in the main street?"

She blinked at him through the steam from a pot on the cooker behind her. With her wild unkempt hair, her thin face and red eyes, she looked like one of the witches who had appeared to the other Macbeth.

"Aye, there's some o' those," she said.

"Like who?"

"Like Hugh McPhee. He went on and on about them."

"And where can I find him?"

"Down at the fishing shop by the loch."

At the bottom of the main street lay the loch, one of those products of the hydro-electricity board. Hamish could remember his mother telling him about how people had been moved out of their villages to make way for these artificial lochs. But they had all been promised that water power would mean cheap electricity and only found out too late that the resultant electricity was not cheap at all. There was a drowned village under Loch Cnothan at the far end. There was something dismal about these man-made stretches of water, he reflected. There weren't any of the trees and bushes around them that you found in the natural ones. At one end of the loch was a great ugly dam. The sun was already going down when Hamish reached Mr. McPhee's shop.

Mr. McPhee sat like a gnome behind the counter of his dark shop among fishing tackle.

Hamish explained the purpose of his visit. "So what's it got to do with me?" asked Mr. McPhee. He was a small gnarled man with arthritic hands.

"I heard you were against the whole business o' the lights," said Hamish.

" 'Course I was. It was that man, Sinclair. Get's hisself elected tae the council and afore you know it, he's got an order for the lights."

"So you weren't objecting on religious grounds?"

"No, you'll need tae go tae Bessie Ward for that. She says the lights are the devil's beacons."

"And where will I find her?"

"Her cottage is at the top o' the main street. It's called Crianlarich."

"Right, I'll try her."

Back up the main street. It was bitter cold and the light was fading fast. He found a small bungalow with the legend CRIANLARICH done in pokerwork on a small wooden board hung over the door on two chains.

He rang the doorbell, which played a parody of Big Ben.

"What is it? Is it my sister, Annie?" asked a solid-looking matron on seeing a uniformed policeman.

"No, nothing like that," said Hamish soothingly. "I am asking questions about the missing Christmas lights."

"Whoever did it was doing the work of the Lord," she said. "You'd best come in."

Hamish followed her into a highly disciplined living room. Church magazines on a low table were arranged in neat squares. Brass objects on the mantel glittered and shone. Cushions were plumped up. Against the outside streetlights, the windows sparkled. The room was cold.

Hamish took off his cap and balanced it on his knees. "I am asking various prominent residents of Cnothan if they might have any idea who did it," began Hamish.

"I neither know nor care." Mrs. Ward sat down opposite him. Her tight tweed skirt rucked up over her thick legs, showing the embarrassed Hamish support hose ending in long pink knickers, those old-fashioned kind with elastic at the bottoms. "The Lord moves in mysterious ways," she added sententiously.

Hamish was about to point out that the Lord did not break padlocks but did not want to offend her. "You look like a verra intelligent woman tae me," he said. Mrs. Ward preened and a coquettish look appeared in her eyes as she surveyed the tall policeman with the hazel eyes and flaming red hair. "Have there be any strangers around here?"

"There's some come and go for the forestry. It's all the fault of that awful man, Sinclair. You know the reason he forced through the collection for the lights? Because he sold them."

"But if there was enough in the collection for the lights," said Hamish, "it follows that some of the people here want them."

"I blame the incomers," she snapped. "God-less lot."

Hamish did not bother asking who the in-comers were. She probably meant people who had settled in Cnothan during the last twenty years. Once a newcomer, always a newcomer. That's the way things were in Cnothan. And you never really got to know anyone in Cnothan. In other villages, he called in at houses on his beat for a chat. He had never dared make an unofficial call on anyone in Cnothan. He surmised that such a respectable house-proud matron would not have anything to do with a theft. He was suddenly anxious to take his leave. But Mrs. Ward pressed him to stay for tea and he weakly agreed.

After he left, he took in great gulps of fresh air outside. He felt he had been trapped in that glittering living room forever. He decided to go back to Lochdubh.

In friendly Lochdubh where everyone gos-siped freely, he would have more chance of picking up news of any strangers in the area. He was sure it was the work of strangers. Surely even the most rabid Calvinist would not stoop to crime.

Back in Lochdubh, he parked the Land Rover and walked along to the doctor's cot-tage. Angela Brodie, the doctor's wife, an-

swered the door to him. "Come in, Hamish," she said, putting a wisp of hair back from her thin face. "I'm just decorating the Christmas tree."

"I'm glad someone in Lochdubh has a Christmas tree," remarked Hamish.

"Come on, Hamish, you know a lot of us have them behind closed doors." She led the way into the cluttered sitting room. The tree was half decorated and Angela's cats were having a great game swiping at the brightly colored glass balls with their paws. Angela gave a cluck of annoyance and scooped up the cats and carried them out to the kitchen.

"So what have you been up to?" she asked when she returned.

Hamish told her about the theft of the Cnothan lights.

"There was a lot of feeling against having the lights by some of the older residents," said Angela. "Might not one of them have taken them?"

"No, I don't think so. You see a large Christmas tree was taken as well. If someone wanted to stop the lights and tree being put up for religious reasons, then they'd probably have smashed the lights and chopped up the tree. Someone's probably down in the streets of Inverness or somewhere like that trying to sell them. In fact, when I get back to the police station, I'll phone the police in Inverness and Strathbane and ask them to keep a lookout for the missing lights."

Hamish passed a pleasant hour helping Angela with the decorations and then went back to the police station. He went into the office and played back the messages on the answering machine. There was a curt one from the bane of his life, Detective Chief Inspector Blair, asking him to phone immediately on his return.

Hamish rang police headquarters and was put through to Blair.

"Listen, pillock," said Blair with all his usual truculence, "there's some auld biddie in your neck o' the woods, a Mrs. Gallagher."

"What about her? She's only missing a cat."

"Well, find the damn animal. She's complained about you, right to Superintendent Daviot. Says you're lazy and neglecting your duties. Says you're a disgrace to community policing."

Hamish sighed. Community policing were the current buzzwords at Strathbane.

"So you get out there and find that cat, dead or alive."

"Yes."

"Yes, *what*?"

"Yes, sir."

Hamish rang off. He decided to eat first and then tackle the horrible Mrs. Gallagher again.

An hour and a half later, he knocked once more at Mrs. Gallagher's cottage. Frost was glittering on the grass round about and his breath came out in white puffs.

He waited patiently while the locks were unlocked and the bolts were drawn back.

She let him in. He was about to give her a row for having made trouble for him at headquarters, but he noticed she had been crying and his face softened.

"Look, Mrs. Gallagher," he said gently, "I was not neglecting my duties. But you must know what it's like. The cat could be anywhere. And why would anyone break in and steal a cat? And how could anyone break in with all the locks and bolts you have? You even have bolts on the windows."

"Someone did," she said stubbornly.

"Have you ever been burgled afore?"

"No, never."

"So why all the locks and bolts?"

"There's a lot of evil people around. And unintelligent ones, too. If you had any intelligence, you wouldn't still be a policeman."

"I choose to stay a policeman," said Hamish,

"and if you expected that remark to hurt, it didn't." It was amazing how little anyone knew of Mrs. Gallagher, he reflected, even though she had been in Lochdubh longer than himself. But then she was damned as a nasty old woman and that was that. It must be a lonely life and she had been crying over the loss of her cat.

"Let's start again, Mrs. Gallagher," he said firmly, "and stop the insults or we won't get anywhere. The mystery here, and it iss where I would like to start, is why you bar and bolt yourself in and why you should immediately think that someone had broken in."

She sat very still, her red work-worn hands folded on her aproned lap. "Can't you just find Smoky?" she pleaded at last.

"I'm giving a talk at the school tomorrow and I'll ask the children if they'll help me to look for Smoky. School's nearly finished. But you have not yet answered my question." He looked at her shrewdly. "Who iss it you are afraid of, Mrs. Gallagher?"

She studied him for a long moment with those odd silver eyes of hers. Then she said abruptly, "Will you be taking a dram with me?"

"Aye, that would be grand."

A flash of humor lit her eyes. "I thought you didn't drink on duty."

"Only on a cold winter's night," said Hamish.

She went to a handsome dresser against the wall and took out two glasses and a bottle of malt whisky. She poured two generous measures, gave him one and then sat back down in her chair, cradling her glass.

"Slainte!" said Hamish, raising his glass with the Gallic toast.

"Slainte," she echoed.

The peat fire sent out a puff of aromatic smoke and an old clock on the mantel gave an asthmatic wheeze before chiming out the hour.

"So," said Hamish curiously, "what brought you up here?"

"My father was a farmer. I was brought up on a farm."

"Where?"

"Over near Oban. I knew I could make a go of it myself."

"You must know country people and country ways. Why all the security?"

A little sigh escaped her. "I always thought one day he would come back."

"He?"

"My husband."

"I thought you were a widow."

"I hope I am. It's been a long time."

"Was he violent?"

Again that sigh. "There you have it. Yes."

"Tell me about it."

"No, it's my business. Finish your drink and go."

Hamish studied her. "Was he in prison?"

"Get out of here, you tiresome man. I'm weary."

Hamish finished his drink and stood up.

"Think about it," he said. "There's no use asking the police for help and then withholding information."

But she did not reply or rise from her chair. He stood looking down at her for a few moments and then he put on his cap and let himself out.

His Highland curiosity was rampant. Why had he never stopped before to wonder about Mrs. Gallagher? She would appear in the village from time to time to stock up on groceries. If someone tried to speak to her she would be so cutting and rude that gradually she had come to be left alone. In the morning he would visit one of the older residents and see if he could find out some facts about her mysterious husband.

Chapter Two

*T*he following day, before he was due to talk to the local schoolchildren, he set out to call on Angus Macdonald. Angus was the local seer, credited with having the gift of second sight. Hamish was cynical about the seer's alleged powers, guessing that Angus relied on a fund of local gossip to fuel his predictions.

He went out to the freezer in the shed at the back of the house and took out two trout he had poached in the summer. The seer always expected a present.

The day was cold and crisp and so he decided to walk up the hill at the back of the village to where Angus lived. Hamish thought

25

cynically that Angus kept the interior of his cottage deliberately old-fashioned, from the oil lamps to the blackened kettle on its chain over the peat fire. His fame had spread far and wide. The dark, old-fashioned living room, Hamish was sure, added to the legends about Angus's gifts.

"It's yourself, Hamish," said Angus, looking more than ever like one of the minor prophets with his shaggy grey hair and long beard.

"Brought you some trout for your tea, Angus."

"Fine, fine. Chust put them down on the counter there. A dram?"

"Better not, Angus. I'm going to give a talk to the schoolchildren and I don't want the smell o' whisky on my breath."

"Sit yourself down and tell me what brings ye."

"Now, now," mocked Hamish, "I thought the grand seer like yourself wouldnae even have to ask."

Angus leaned back and half closed his eyes. "She isnae coming back this Christmas."

Hamish scowled horribly. He knew Angus was referring to the once love of his life, Priscilla Halburton-Smythe.

"I didn't come about that," said Hamish crossly. "Mrs. Gallagher's cat is missing." He opened his notebook, took out the black-and-white photograph of Smoky and handed it to the seer.

"It iss grey and white, that cat," said the seer.

"You've seen it?"

"No, I chust know."

"So tell me about Mrs. Gallagher. I wasn't around when she came to Lochdubh. There's something about her husband. Know anything about that?"

"I thought she was a widow."

"So you don't know everything, Angus."

"No one can know everything," said Angus huffily. "You will need to give me a bittie o' time to consult the spirits."

"Aye, you do that," said Hamish, heading for the door.

The seer's voice followed him. "I find a bit o' steak does wonders for the memory."

Hamish swung round. "I gave you two trout!"

"Aye, but there's nothing like a bit of steak for helping an auld man's memory."

"Aren't you frightened of the mad cow's disease?"

"Not me," said Angus with a grin.

"Aye, you've probably got it already," muttered Hamish as he walked down the frosty hill.

The village school only catered for young children. The older ones were bused to the high school in Strathbane. There was a new school-teacher, a Miss Maisie Pease, and it was she who had suggested that Hamish talk to the children. She was a small, neat woman with shiny black hair, a rather large prominent nose and fine brown eyes like peaty water. Hamish judged her to be in her thirties.

"Now, Officer," she began.

"Hamish."

"Well, Hamish it is, and I'm Maisie. I feel that children are never too young to learn about the perils of drugs, as well as all the usual cautions about not talking to strangers."

"Right. Are the children ready for me?"

"They're all in the main classroom."

Hamish walked with her along a corridor to the classroom. As he neared it, he could hear the row of unsupervised children. When he pushed open the door, there came a frantic scrabbling of small pupils rushing back to their desks. Maisie followed him in.

"This is P. C. Macbeth, children," she said. "I want you to sit quietly and pay attention."

Hamish looked round the faces of twenty-four children, ranging in ages from five to eleven years old, rosy-cheeked Highland faces with bright eyes.

He started off by talking about the evils of bullying and of stealing. He warned them against talking to strangers or accepting lifts from strangers and then moved on to the subject of drugs. Not so very long ago, he reflected, such a talk would have been unnecessary. But drugs had found their way even up into the Highlands of Scotland. He then asked for questions.

After a polite silence, one little boy put up his hand. "Is wacky baccie bad?"

Hamish, identifying "wacky baccie" as pot, said, "Yes, it is. It's against the law. But a lot of people will tell you there's nothing to it. It's better than booze. But it's not. You can get sicker quicker and it destroys short-term memory. Just say no."

Another boy put up his hand. "My brither wants to know where he can get Viagra."

"Ask Dr. Brodie," said Hamish. The boy relapsed, sniggering with his friends. So much for the innocence of youth, thought Hamish.

He then asked them what Santa Claus was bringing them. He was answered by a chorus of voices calling out that they wanted dolls or mountain bikes or dogs or cats. Hamish was glad that the children were not going to be denied Christmas, however Calvinistic the parents, although in the Lochdubh way, it would probably be celebrated behind closed doors.

"I'm going to talk to you now about pets," said Hamish. He thought briefly of his own dog, Towser, long dead, and felt a pang of sadness. "Don't ask your parents for a dog or a cat unless you're very sure what looking after an animal entails. A dog, for instance, has to be house-trained, walked and fed, possibly for the next fifteen years of your life. A cat even longer. It's cruel to want an animal as a sort of toy. If I were you, I'd wait until you're a bit older. Dogs have to be properly trained up here or you'll have some animal worrying the sheep.

"While I remember," he said, "someone or some people have stolen the Christmas lights that were meant to decorate the street in Cnothan. I want you to let me know if you hear anything about strangers in the Cnothan area. There's a bit o' detective work for you. Ask your older brothers or sisters or your parents and if there's anything at all, let me know. Also, Mrs. Gallagher has lost a cat. I'm going to pass round a photograph of the cat and I want you all to study it carefully and then search for this cat. There'll be a reward."

Schoolteacher Maisie then showed him out. "I see you don't have the classroom decorated," said Hamish.

"We were going to make some paper decorations but you know how it is. Some of the parents objected. They said they didn't mind giving their children a present, but that they were against what they call pagan celebrations. It's hard on the children because they all watch television and they are all in love with the idea of a Christmas tree and lights and all those things. Oh, well, it's only at Christmas that they get stroppy. Other times, this must be the nicest place in the Highlands."

"It is that," said Hamish. "Maybe you'd like to have a bite of dinner with me one night?"

She looked startled and then smiled. "Are you asking me out on a date?"

Hamish thought gloomily about his unlucky love life and said quickly, "Chust a friendly meal."

"Then that would be nice."

"What about tomorrow evening? At the Italian restaurant? About eight?"

"I'll be there."

"Grand," said Hamish, giving her a dazzling smile.

Mrs. Wellington, the minister's wife, was just arriving and heard the exchange. She waited until Hamish had left and then said in her booming voice, "I feel I should warn you against that man, Miss Pease."

"Oh, why?" asked the schoolteacher. "He's not married, is he?"

"No, more's the pity. He is a philanderer."

"Dear me."

"He was engaged to Priscilla Halburton-Smythe, daughter of Colonel Halburton-Smythe who owns the Tommel Castle Hotel. He broke off the engagement and broke her heart."

Miss Pease had already heard quite a lot of Lochdubh gossip, and the gossips had it the other way round, that Priscilla had broken Hamish's heart.

"Oh, well," said Miss Pease, "he can't do much to me over dinner."

"That's what you think," said Mrs. Wellington awfully. "Now about the Sunday school . . ."

Hamish walked along the waterfront and met one of the fishermen, Archie Maclean. The locals said that Archie's wife boiled all his clothes, and certainly they always looked too tight for his small figure, as if every one had been shrunk and then starched and ironed. The creases in his trousers were like knife blades and his tweed jacket was stretched tightly across his stooped shoulders.

"Getting ready for Christmas, Archie?" Hamish hailed him.

"When wass there effer the Christmas in our house?" grumbled Archie.

"I didn't think the wife was religious."

"No, but herself says she's having none of those nasty Christmas trees shedding needles in her house, nor any of that nasty tinsel. You ken we've the only washhouse left in Lochdubh?"

Hamish nodded. The washhouse at the back of Archie's cottage had been used in the old days before washing machines. It contained a huge copper basin set in limestone brick where the clothes were once boiled on wash-day.

"Well, the neighbors have been dropping by tae use it tae boil up their cloutie dumplings. But dae ye think I'll get a piece. Naw!"

Cloutie dumpling, that Scottish Christmas special, is a large pudding made of raisins, sultanas, dates, flour and suet, all boiled in a large cloth or pillowcase. Some families still kept silver sixpences from the old days before decimal coinage to drop into the pudding. Large and brown and steaming and rich, it was placed on the table at Christmas and decorated with a sprig of holly. It was so large it lasted for weeks, slices of it even being served fried with bacon for breakfast.

"In fact," said Archie, "the only one what's offered me a piece is Mrs. Brodie."

"Angela? The doctor's wife?"

"Herself."

"But Angela can't cook!"

"I know that fine. But herself says she's going to try this year. Herself says it's surely chust like a scientific experiment. You measure out the exact amounts."

"It never works with Angela," said Hamish. "Her cakes are like rocks. Come for a dram, Archie. I've been talking to the schoolchildren and it's thirsty work."

They walked into the Lochdubh bar together.

When they were settled at a corner table with glasses of whisky, Hamish asked, "Do you know any gossip about Mrs. Gallagher?"

"Her, out the Cnothan road? Why?"

"I've been thinking. We all know her as a sour-faced bitch. But why?"

"Cos she's a sour-faced bitch. Postman says she's got the place like Fort Knox wi' locks and bolts."

"I mean, what soured her? Was she always like that?"

"I think so. Good sheep. Doesn't have dogs. She just whistles to the sheep, different whistles and they do what she wants. She had one friend."

"Who?"

"I don't know if the woman iss still alive. She bought the croft from her. Mrs. Dunwiddy. She went to live with a daughter in Inverness. Wait a bit. Maybe two years back now, someone says to me that Mrs. Dunwiddy had a stroke and she's in an old folks home in Inverness. What's she done?"

"She done nothing. She thinks someone's pinched her cat."

"Gone wild probably or the fox got it."

"That's what I told her."

"So what d'ye want to know about her for?"

"Curious. That's all. I think she's a verra frightened woman."

"Listen, Hamish, if I lived up there and never spoke to a body except to do a deal for sheep at the sales at Lairg, I'd get frightened as well."

"I think there's more to it than that. Oh, and if you hear of someone selling Christmas lights, let me know. Cnothan's had theirs stolen."

"There's a lot o' Free Presbyterians o'er there."

The great essayist Bernard Levin once described the Free Presbyterian as the sort of people who thought that if they did not keep the blankets tight over their feet at night, the pope would nip down the chimney and bite their toes.

"Maybe," said Hamish. "But I doubt it. The lights were taken along with a tree out of that shed at the community hall. The padlock was smashed. Any loose elements roaming the countryside?"

"Haven't heard. Don't get them in the winter."

"If you hear anything, let me know."

Hamish returned to the police station to collect the Land Rover and drive to Cnothan.

He was once more examining the shed when Mr. Sinclair came up to him. "You're not wearing gloves," he accused.

"Why should I?"

"You'll be destroying fingerprints."

Hamish sighed. He knew Strathbane would not send out a team of forensic experts to help solve the mere theft of a Christmas tree and lights.

Ignoring Mr. Sinclair, he set out, stooped over the ground, following the trail of pine needles. He went through the gate into the common grazing ground. No more needles. There must have been more than one. He could imagine them getting it over the gate and then lifting it onto their shoulders. He set off up the hill, doubled over, studying the ground. He guessed they would go fast and in a straight line.

Mr. Sinclair stood watching him until the tall

figure had disappeared over the crest of the hill. "That man's a useless fool," he said to the frosty air. "It's a pity Sergeant Macgregor is off ill." He quite forgot that Sergeant Macgregor would have considered such a trivial theft not worth bothering about. Mr. Sinclair was feeling particularly righteous. He had supplied a new set of lights, which were being put up on the main street at that moment, and he had not charged for them.

Hamish spent the rest of the day searching over the common grazing ground until he came upon the peat stacks on the other side of the hill. There, in muddy, watery ground, he came across tire tracks. They could have been made by one of the locals, but as he studied them, he saw a little cluster of pine needles and some marks made by, he thought, running shoes. He counted the different footprints. Four sets of them. They'd probably come to thieve peats and then thought they might stroll over towards the village to see if there was anything they could lift. He stood studying the prints, trying to build up a mental picture of the robbers. There had been a lot of petty theft over towards Lairg, tools lifted from garden sheds, things like that. He decided to put a full report into headquarters and ask for a printout of areas of recent petty theft in Sutherland. That way he might find the area they were operating from. Because of the pettiness of the other thefts, not much police work had gone into finding the culprits. They would possibly be unemployed, hard drinkers, the sort who preyed on farmhouses and cottages during agricultural shows when they knew people would be away from home.

As Hamish prepared a meal for himself that evening, he thought about the schoolteacher. It would be pleasant to talk to someone new. He stopped, about to drain the potatoes into the colander. There had been something wrong in that classroom. He had picked up at one point a little atmosphere of fear. Then he shrugged. He would ask Maisie Pease about it.

The following morning, he decided to run down to Inverness and do some last-minute Christmas shopping. The presents he had already bought for his family were waiting at the police station, but he needed to buy a few little presents for his friends in the village. He would phone in regularly to his answering machine just in case anything cropped up.

It was ten o'clock when he set off and the sun was just struggling up over the horizon. It was one of those unexpectedly mild winter days when a west wind blows in over the Gulf Stream.

As all the main stores in Inverness are crammed into the centre of the town, he found the main street as full of shoppers as ever. Inverness was always busy. Finally, when he had accumulated a supply of various presents, he returned to the police Land Rover. He phoned his answering machine but there were no messages. It was then he remembered Mrs. Gallagher's friend, Mrs. Dunwiddy.

He went to the central police station and asked if he could use the phone. Hamish had his mobile phone with him, but he wanted to phone around to old folks homes in the area and so he wanted a warm desk, a phone book and a police phone where the cost would not appear on his own phone bill.

On the sixth try, he landed lucky. Yes, they had a Mrs. Dunwiddy, but she was very frail and rambled most of the time. Nonetheless, he said he would call and see her.

He found the old folks home out on old Beauly Road. What was it like, he wondered as he parked in the gravelled drive, to end up in one of these places when you were old? He walked inside. There was a lounge to the right where several elderly people sat staring at a television set. The lounge was decorated with glittering colored chains of tinsel. An overdecorated Christmas tree stood beside the television set, dripping with glass balls and tinsel. Somehow, the festive decorations made the television watchers seem older, more frail and forgotten.

He went to the reception desk, produced his identification and asked for Mrs. Dunwiddy. "She has a few good days still," said a brisk woman, "but I don't think this is one of them. She's in her room. I'll take you along."

"Do any of her family visit her?" asked Hamish as he followed her along a thickly carpeted corridor.

"She's got a son and a daughter. They don't come often. You know how it is. This place is expensive and these days, people feel they've done their duty by paying out. Sad. Here we are. Visitor for you, dear."

Mrs. Dunwiddy sat in a wheelchair by the window. She was staring out with blank eyes at a bleak winter lawn at the back of the building.

"I won't be long," said Hamish. He pulled up a chair and sat down next to Mrs. Dunwiddy. The woman who had ushered him in said, "There's a bell on the wall if you need anything, Officer." Then she left.

"Mrs. Dunwiddy," began Hamish. Her old eyes did not flicker.

"I don't know if you remember," said Hamish, "but you sold your croft and house to a Mrs. Gallagher."

Silence.

"I'm worried about Mrs. Gallagher," said Hamish. "She lives up there by herself, been on her own since she moved in. She's got the place bolted and barred. What is she frightened of?"

Silence.

"I thought you might know something, that she might have said something."

She could have been carved out of rock.

Hamish gave a little sigh. He must ask if there was any pattern to her good days and try again. On the other hand, it was a lot of trouble to go to for a nasty woman. He decided there was nothing he could get out of her that day. He rose to leave.

"Cat," she said suddenly.

Hamish turned. One frail trembling hand had risen and was pointing at the window. He looked out. A black cat was sliding slowly on its belly towards a starling which was tugging at a worm. Hamish banged on the window and the cat fled.

Hamish sat down again. "Mrs. Gallagher?" he said gently. "Remember her?"

"Alice," she said, her voice like dry autumn leaves blowing across a tarmac road.

"Alice Gallagher?"

"Bastard."

"Who?"

"Said he beat her. Said she ran away."

"Her husband?"

"Have you washed your face, Johnny? You're going to be late for school."

Hamish tried to get more out of her but her brain had retreated to the past. He quietly left.

As he crossed the hall, he once more looked in the lounge. There they sat with the television set blaring. What a Christmas!

He had a sudden idea. He went back to the desk. "Miss—?"

"Mrs. Kirk," she said.

"Well, Mrs. Kirk, is anything ever done to brighten up those folks in the lounge?"

"They have the television."

"I just thought of something. Could I arrange a wee concert for them, for Christmas day?"

"I don't see why not. Could you wait and I'll get our director."

After a few moments, Hamish was ushered into an office where a small, bespectacled man was sitting behind a desk.

He rose and held out his hand. "I am John Wilson. You were saying something to Mrs. Kirk here about a concert?"

"Aye, just an idea. For Christmas."

"What sort of concert?"

"I know a retired couple, used to be on the halls. They can still play and sing all the old songs. Old people like that."

"I'll need to look into our budget," he began fussily.

"No charge."

"Well, in that case, it does seem a good idea. In fact, we have other homes like this. If they're any good, we might employ them to do the rounds."

"Oh, they're good," said Hamish. "I'll arrange it for the afternoon of Christmas day."

"That's very kind of you, Officer. May I ask why you are doing this?"

Hamish smiled. "Because it's Christmas."

He then drove to a housing estate at the north of the town, home of Charlie and Bella Underwood.

Bella answered the door. She was in her seventies, but her hair was dyed a flaming red and she was heavily made up. "Hamish!" she cried. "God, it's been ages. Come in, darling! Charlie, it's Hamish!"

A dapper little man came out to meet them. "What brings you, Hamish?"

"It should be a friendly call," said Hamish

when they were all seated over a fat teapot in the Underwoods' kitchen. "But I'm afraid it's because I've got a business proposition for you."

"Business?" asked Bella. "We've been out of the business for a while."

Hamish explained about the old folks home. "You see," he said, "you know all the old sing-along songs. Can you still perform?"

"Course we can," said Bella. "You're a gem, Hamish."

"I'll be paying you for this myself, but if that Mr. Wilson likes you, you could get more work."

"Keep your money, Hamish," said Charlie. "We'll do it for nothing."

Pleased with his outing, Hamish returned to Lochdubh. He would tackle Mrs. Gallagher in the morning. In the meantime, there was his dinner with Maisie to look forward to. He washed and dressed carefully in his one good suit, brushed his flaming red hair until it shone, and then strolled along the waterfront towards the Italian restaurant. Great stars burned in the Sutherland sky overhead and their reflections twinkled in the black sea loch like the missing Christmas decorations.

He pushed open the door of the restaurant and

went in. He was greeted by the waiter, Willie Lamont. Willie, in the heady days when Hamish had been elevated to police sergeant before being demoted again, had been Hamish's sidekick, but he had married the beautiful daughter of the restaurant owner and left the police force.

Willie conducted him to a table at the window. "I'm waiting for a lady," said Hamish. "I'll order when she arrives."

Willie whipped out a bottle of cleaner and began scrubbing at the table. "The table was clean already," protested Hamish, remembering how Willie, a fanatical cleaner, had scrubbed out the police station instead of paying attention to his duties.

"It's a real grand cleaner," said Willie. "It's called 'SCCRUBB.' I sent away for it."

"Willie, Willie, it's taking the polish off the table."

"Oh, michty-me, so it iss. I'll just get some polish."

"No," said Hamish firmly. "Leave it until we've eaten."

Willie's face twisted in anguish. "Just a wee scoosh o' wax," he pleaded.

"Not even one." Hamish rose to his feet. "Here's my lady."

Maisie Pease joined him. "This is very nice," she said, looking around.

She sat down in a chair and then shrank back as Willie darted up to the table and shot a spray of liquid wax from a canister and then began polishing fiercely.

"Go away, Willie!" shouted Hamish. "And bring the menus." Muttering, Willie went off.

"What a strange waiter," said Maisie.

"Oh, he's all right. Just a bit keen on cleaning."

They were the only customers in the restaurant. They ordered food and wine, but the hovering presence of Willie unnerved Maisie. She knocked over a glass of wine, she dropped spaghetti on the table and dropped her bread roll on the floor, and there was Willie each time, mopping and polishing and complaining. Hamish at last stood up and marched Willie into the kitchen and threatened to punch his head if he came near the table again unless they called for him.

"I'm sorry about that," said Hamish. "He'll leave us alone now."

"Tell me all about Lochdubh," said Maisie. "I'm just getting to know it and the people."

So Hamish told her about the people in the village, and she watched his thin attractive face and wondered if he was the philanderer that Mrs. Wellington had said he was.

Then Hamish said, "I had a feeling when I

was giving that talk that someone was frightened. Just a feeling. Any bullying going on?"

"Not that I know of. But it's early days for me. It could just be that maybe some of the children were lying."

"What about?"

"I don't know if it's true, but some of them come from very strict religious homes. So when you asked them what Santa Claus was bringing them, they all replied, but in some of the homes, there won't be any Christmas presents."

"That's sad. I know some of them are against Christmas but I didnae think they would take it out on their children."

"I'll ask about."

They talked of other things and then Hamish walked her back to her cottage, which was attached to the schoolhouse. She smiled and thanked him for dinner. He smiled back and then turned and walked away.

Maisie went slowly indoors. He hadn't even tried to kiss her. He hadn't suggested a second date. Philanderer indeed!

Chapter Three

*H*amish did not want to visit Mrs. Gallagher. But the idea that someone had been living in solitude and fear on his beat nagged at him. The wind had come back and as he drove off, a ragged cloud of crows rose up from the field behind the police station and scattered out over the loch. Low clouds scurried over the mountaintops. Hamish wondered if the Romans had held their Saturnalia at just this time as a sort of drunken wake to the death of the year. On such a day it seemed as if the grass would never grow again or the sun shine.

Mrs. Gallagher was out in the fields. As he approached, he could see her striding back towards the house. She had seen his arrival and waited at the door for him.

"Well?" she demanded.

"No news."

"Then I have no time for you."

"I would like to speak to you for a little bit."

"Why?"

"I want to talk to you about your husband."

She ducked her head suddenly to hide her face. She stood like that for a long moment and then took a ring of keys out of the pocket of her old tweed coat and began to unlock the door.

"Come in," she said curtly.

Hamish removed his cap and followed her in. She turned to face him. "What about my husband?"

"Can we sit down?"

She nodded. She took off her coat and hung it on a peg by the door.

"It's like this," said Hamish when he was seated. "I have reason to believe that you are still afraid of your husband."

"What's that got to do with my missing cat?"

Hamish studied her and then with a sudden flash of Highland intuition, he said, "For some reason, you live in fear of him, and when Smoky disappeared, you were frightened he had come back to take your cat away. That's the sort of thing he would do—destroy something you loved."

Her face was now a muddy color. "You know him," she whispered. "You've met him."

"No. But did you never think of appealing to me for help? You could have taken out an injunction against him. Was he ever in prison?"

There was a long silence. The wind howled around the low croft house like a banshee.

Then she said, "He was arrested for armed robbery. We were living in Glasgow at the time. I saw my chance to get free and took it. My mother had died and left me money. I managed to keep that fact from him. I drew out all the money and came up here."

"Look, what's his full name?"

"Why?"

"Because," said Hamish patiently, "I can check up on him. I can find out where he is and what he's doing. He could be dead. Think of that. The man could be dead and here are you, talking to no one and living scared."

"Hugh," she said. "Hugh Gallagher."

"Last address?"

"Springburn Road, number five-A."

Hamish scribbled rapidly in his notebook. "And when was he arrested?"

"In nineteen seventy-eight. In March. It was the eighteenth when they came for him."

"Right, I'll get onto that right away."

He stood up. She rose as well and clutched at his dark blue regulation sweater. "You won't let him know where I am."

"No, no," he said soothingly. "I've told the schoolchildren to help look for your cat, so if you see any of them about, don't be chasing them off."

She sank back in her chair and covered her face with her hands.

"You should have friends," said Hamish.

"You can't trust anyone," she said from behind her hands.

Hamish left and drove back to the police station. He phoned Strathclyde Police Headquarters in Glasgow and put in a request to find out what had become of an armed robber called Hugh Gallagher, arrested in March of 1978 for armed robbery.

They said they would phone him back. He fed his sheep and hens and decided to drive up to the Tommel Castle Hotel to see if there was any news of Priscilla Halburton-Smythe.

He was welcomed by the manager, Mr. Johnston. "Come to mooch a cup of coffee, Hamish?"

"Aye, that would be grand."

"Come into the office. Herself won't be home for Christmas."

Hamish blushed. "I didn't come here to ask that. But I thought she would come home to see her parents."

"She's working for some big computer firm and they've sent her to New York."

So far away, thought Hamish. So very far away.

"So how's business?" he asked with well-manufactured cheeriness.

"Business is booming. We're fully booked for the Christmas period."

"No news about the old Lochdubh Hotel down by the harbour?"

"Some Japanese put in a bid but then the Japanese recession hit. Then other folks seem to think there isn't room up here for more than one hotel."

"It's a grand building. Could do for a school."

"So how's policing?"

"Nice and quiet."

"No juicy murders for Christmas?"

"God forbid. I've got the case of the missing cat and the case of the missing Christmas lights at Cnothan."

"Ach, Cnothan! That's such a sour wee place they probably took away the lights themselves, them that thinks Christmas is sinful."

"I think it was youths. Petty theft. Anyway,

Cnothan may be a sour place but at least they wanted to put up some decorations. Look at Lochdubh, as black as the loch."

"Well, Mr. Wellington the minister was all for putting up a tree this year on the waterfront but he came up against Josiah Anderson."

"What! Him that lives in that big Victorian house?"

"The same. A real Bible basher. I'm sorry for that wee daughter o' his."

"He's got a wee daughter?"

"So you don't know everything. Josiah and his wife were trying for years to have children."

"Probably didn't know how to go about it," said Hamish maliciously. "They should have asked me and I'd have given them a map."

"Anyway, the wife went down to Inverness for the fertility treatment and she had a girl. Josiah was fifty when the bairn was born and the wife, Mary, forty-five. The wee girl, Morag, she must be about nine now. What a life for her, they're that strict. No presents for her."

"She goes to the village school?"

"Aye."

"I gave a talk to the kids there and asked them what Santa was bringing them and they were all expecting something."

"What child wants to be different from the others?" asked Mr. Johnston.

"What does Morag Anderson look like?"

"Like a waif. All eyes. And clean. Oh, so clean. I think they scrub her every morning."

Hamish's hazel eyes narrowed. "Sounds like cruelty to me. I'll have a talk to the school-teacher."

"I've heard you've been romancing her — dinner at the Italian place."

"Have I no private life?" mourned Hamish.

"Aye, well, if you'd wanted a private life you wouldn't have chosen to live in Lochdubh. But I'm in a generous mood. If you want to take her for lunch, I'll let you have it on the house."

Hamish drank his coffee, then headed for the schoolhouse. He looked at his watch. School would be breaking up any minute for the Christmas holidays. The children were singing carols, their voices carried towards him on the wind. He waited in the Land Rover until he saw them streaming out. Then he got out and went into the schoolhouse.

Maisie Pease was clearing up papers on her desk. She looked up and blushed when she saw him. "Why, Hamish! What brings you?"

Ask me out again, a voice inside her was urging. But Hamish perched on the side of her desk and said, "You've got a pupil here, Morag Anderson."

"Yes, and I won't believe for a moment she's in trouble. She's my star pupil."

"No, she's not in any police trouble. I heard an unsettling piece of gossip about her parents, that's all. Seems they're a bit too strict. No Christmas for Morag."

"I can't really do anything about that, Hamish. I would be interfering with their religious beliefs."

"Nonetheless, I would like to talk to them."

So you're not going to ask me out, thought Maisie huffily. "I can't stop you," she said curtly. "Go ahead. Have a word with them if you want."

"I thought maybe since it's just noon you would like to come with me and then we could have a bite of lunch."

"At the Italian place?"

"No, I'll take you to the Tommel Castle Hotel."

"Oh, Hamish. That's so expensive."

"Think nothing of it. My treat."

Maisie's face was now flushed with pleasure. "I'll get my coat."

Most of the houses in Lochdubh were eighteenth century when the then Duke of Sutherland had hoped to expand the fishing industry. But there were a few large Victorian villas built in the last century when the lesser orders copied their queen by having holiday homes in Scotland. But now that people who could afford it usually preferred their holiday homes to be in Spain or some other sunny country, the villas were no longer holiday homes but residences of the middle class. Josiah Anderson owned a clothing factory in Strathbane. Hamish opened the double iron garden gate and ushered Maisie inside.

"What are the parents like?" he asked in a low voice.

"A wee bit severe. I've met them on parents day. Morag always has top marks so I've never had any reason to talk much to them."

Hamish rang the brass bell set into the wall beside the door. When he found himself looking down at Mrs. Anderson when she opened the door, he was surprised. He realized he had seen her about the village, had exchanged a few words with her in the general store, knew she was Mrs. Anderson. But he had forgotten, and had conjured up a picture of a grim matron.

Mrs. Anderson was small and neat with permed hair and a rosy face. She looked startled at the sight of Hamish. "Nothing wrong?" she cried.

"Just a friendly call," said Hamish.

"Come in. My husband's in the sitting room."

They followed her into the sitting room which was large and dark, high-ceilinged, full of heavy furniture and impeccably clean.

"Josiah," said Mrs. Anderson, "here's our policeman and Miss Pease, Morag's schoolteacher."

He rose to greet them. He was wearing a charcoal grey three-piece suit with a white shirt and striped tie. His black shoes were highly polished. He had thinning grey hair, thick lips, small watchful eyes and tufts of hair sprouting from the nostrils of a large nose.

"What's up?" he asked.

"Just a friendly call," said Hamish again.

"Sit down, sit down, Officer. Mary, get tea."

"It's all right," said Hamish. "We won't be long. We're on our way for lunch."

They all sat down. Hamish looked at Maisie as a signal for her to begin.

"Christmas is very important for little children," said Maisie.

"That is because each year they are brainwashed into a state of greed," said Mr. Anderson.

"I don't think that's true," said Hamish. "There's an innocent magic about it. I hope Morag isn't going to be left out."

Mrs. Anderson opened her mouth to say

something, but Mr. Anderson held up his hand. "Our Morag is a sensible girl. She knows such things as Santa Claus and presents are pagan flummery."

"It's a bit of a burden to put on a wee girl," protested Hamish. "All her friends at school will be excited about it."

"I see you will need to talk to Morag herself. Get her, Mary."

Mrs. Anderson went out to the foot of the stairs and called, "Morag, come down here a minute."

They waited until Morag came into the room. She looked at Hamish and her face turned white and her eyes dilated.

"Now, then, Morag," said her mother quickly, "there's nothing to be afraid of. Constable Macbeth and Miss Pease have called because they are worried you might be feeling left out of the Christmas celebrations."

"I beg your pardon?" said Morag faintly.

In the rest of the modern world, when people didn't understand what you were saying, they said "What?" or "Excuse me?" But in the Highlands, they still used the old-fashioned "I beg your pardon?"

"They're worried that you might feel different from the other children because we don't have anything to do with Christmas."

Morag stood there and slowly color returned to her face. "Oh, no," she said softly. "I don't bother about it."

"Are you sure?" asked Maisie.

"Oh, yes."

"There you are," said Mr. Anderson. "You're a good girl, Morag. You can go to your room." He turned to Maisie. "You may think we're a bit hard about Christmas but we have our religion and we live by it. Morag gets plenty of presents on her birthday."

Maisie looked helplessly at Hamish. He indicated to her that they should leave. But as Mrs. Anderson was showing them out, he turned and looked down at her. "Did you never think it might not be a good idea to let Morag make up her own mind about what she wants to believe in when she's older?"

"No, children need to be guided young. As you can see, she is not troubled at all. She has everything a little girl could desire. She has her own room and bathroom and a little sitting room at the top of the house where she can entertain her friends."

"Does she bring friends home?"

A shadow crossed Mrs. Anderson's face. "Not yet, but she will when she is older. She is a very happy, self-sufficient girl. She does all the housekeeping for her part of the house herself. She volunteered. And she even asked if she could cook some meals for herself."

They thanked her and left. As they drove towards the Tommel Castle Hotel, Hamish said, "That was one very frightened little girl."

"People are always frightened by the sight of a policeman."

"Not of me. She saw me in the classroom and I was with you. I thought for a minute she was going to faint."

"I tell you what it could be. Mr. Patel? He sometimes catches little kids stealing sweets from his store. He doesn't call you, he calls me. I see the parents and the matter's settled. Maybe Morag took something and thought the forces of law and order had descended on her. I mean, imagine her parents' reaction if they found their precious child was a thief."

"Could be. There's such a thing as a child being *too* good. But her strict upbringing doesn't seem to have affected her studies."

"No, she's bright and she likes learning. She has a terrific imagination. She writes very colorful essays."

"I'd like to see some of them."

"You're worrying too much, Hamish. How did you ever get time to catch all those murderers I've heard you arrested if you fret so much over a wee schoolgirl?"

"I'm curious," was all Hamish would say.

When they entered the dining room of the hotel, the maître d', Mr. Jenkins, who had once been butler to the Halburton-Smythes, ushered them to a table. "You're to have the cock a leekie soup, followed by the venison," he said. He flicked a napkin open and spread it on Maisie's lap and departed.

"How odd," said Maisie. "Don't they give you a menu here?"

"It must be a set meal for lunch."

Maisie glanced around. Some diners were holding large leather-bound menus. She decided not to comment on it. Perhaps the maître d' knew that Hamish liked the set menu.

"Would you like some wine?" asked Hamish.

"That would be nice. Can you drink and drive?"

"Not really and I shouldn't be driving you around in the police vehicle, either. But I'll get us a couple of glasses. Excuse me a minute."

Hamish went through to the hotel office and said to Mr. Johnston, "It's kind of you to give me lunch. I want to order wine but that snobby scunner Jenkins'll make a fuss."

Mr. Johnson laughed. "You don't want your date to know you aren't paying for it. Okay, I'll bring you something."

Hamish returned and sat down. Soon Mr. Johnston arrived, bearing a bottle of claret which he deftly opened. Hamish introduced him to Maisie. "We keep a special claret just for Hamish," said Mr. Johnston.

"I hope you're not going to live on baked beans for a month after paying for this," said Maisie.

"Och, no. I've got a bit saved up." Hamish thought about his bank account, which was sinking rapidly into the red after his Christmas shopping. Maisie was just gathering courage after they had finished their soup to invite Hamish out for a meal, when he said suddenly, "Are you doing anything on Christmas day? I mean, are you going to be with your family?"

"No, my parents are dead and my sister's in Australia. I was going to cook a small turkey and toast myself. Would you like to join me?"

"If you'll join me in something first." He told her about the old folks home in Inverness and ended by saying, "I thought of dropping down there on Christmas day to hear the concert."

"Of course I'll come," said Maisie delight-edly, "and then when we get back you can join me for Christmas dinner."

Hamish beamed at her. It looked as if it was going to be a good Christmas after all.

• • •

In the hotel office, the phone rang. Mr. Johnston picked it up. "It's me, Priscilla," came Priscilla Halburton-Smythe's voice. "How are things?"

"We're fully booked. Do you want me to get your father or mother for you?"

"No, I spoke to them yesterday." There was a pause and then Priscilla said, "I've just phoned the police station. Hamish isn't there. I didn't bother leaving a message, but you haven't seen him, have you?"

"Yes, he's right here in the dining room."

"Well, if I could . . ."

"He's having lunch with his lady friend."

"Oh, who's she?"

"Maisie Pease, a right pretty lass, the new schoolteacher. I think there'll be wedding bells soon. Do you want me to get Hamish to the phone?"

"No," said Priscilla quickly. "Don't bother." She asked some more questions about the hotel and then rang off.

The manager looked at the now silent phone. He felt guilty but, on the other hand, he told himself, how was Hamish ever going to get over Priscilla if she kept jerking his chain?

Hamish drove Maisie back to her cottage and then made his way back to the police station. He switched on the answering machine. The first was only a silence and then a click as someone rang off. The second was from Strathclyde Police from the policewoman who had been searching the records for Mrs. Gallagher's husband. "I've got something," she said. "Ring me."

Hamish phoned up Glasgow and was put through to her. "I don't know if this is good news or bad, Hamish," she said, "but he's dead."

"That's good news. When and how?"

"He got knifed in a drunken brawl in the Govan area two years ago."

"Thanks," said Hamish. "That wraps that up."

He set off once more, heading towards Mrs. Gallagher's croft. No more lame ducks, Hamish Macbeth, he told himself severely. Give her the good news and then leave her alone, apart from still trying to find out if her cat's about.

"Macbeth!" he called loudly as he knocked on the door.

She opened the door on the chain. "Have you found Smoky?"

"No, but I've got some news for you about your husband. Can I come in?"

She dropped the chain and held open the door.

In the kitchen she turned to face him. "He's dead," said Hamish.

She sat down abruptly as if her legs had

given way. Hamish took off his cap and placed it on the table and sat down opposite her.

"How? When did he die?"

"Two years ago. A drunken fight in Govan. He got knifed."

"Thank you," she said faintly. Then she said, "I'm a silly old woman. If only I'd asked for help before."

"He probably terrorized you. What were you about to get involved with a man like that?"

"I didn't know he was a man like that," she snapped, all her old crustiness returning.

"Like I said, I lived on a farm near Oban with my parents, well, just outside Oban that is. He stopped by one day on his motorcycle. He wanted to know if we did bed-and-breakfast. My mother said, yes, even though we didn't have a sign on the road. She usually only catered for a few regulars who came year after year. He said he would book in for two nights." Her silver eyes grew dreamy as she seemed to look down some long tunnel into a bright past where life had still been innocent.

"He was very good-looking, tall with fair hair. He said he was up from Glasgow. I'd led a very sheltered life but I'd been to the cinema and like the other girls, we were all mad about James Dean. Hugh had this big shiny motor-bike and he wore a leather jacket. He took me to the cinema and dancing. He stayed two weeks instead of two days and by the end of the two weeks, he'd asked me to marry him. I was over the moon. He said he had a good job and worked as a salesman. I wanted a church wedding but Hugh said he was in a rush because he had to get back to his job. My parents were upset, but I was twenty-one so there was nothing they could do to stop me. We got married in the registry office and then he went off to Glasgow and I packed up and followed him down on the train. He'd said his parents were dead. Would you like some tea?"

Hamish shook his head. "His flat was a bit of a shock. It was in a tenement in Springburn, dark and sordid. He said, don't worry, he had something in mind. We'd soon be out of there. Then things began to fall apart. My father phoned and said money from the farm office was missing and only Hugh could have taken it. Of course, I stood up for Hugh and we had a row and he told me never to come back to the farm again until I had come to my senses. Then one day when Hugh was out, his parents came by. Yes, parents! The father was drunk and the mother was a slattern. Hugh came home and threw them out. I asked him why he had lied to me. He said he was ashamed of his parents and that his father used to beat him.

"Oh, I believed him because I wanted to. Then the police came for him. He had stolen the motorbike. He got a short prison sentence and when he came out, he stopped keeping up any front for me. He would get drunk and beat me. And yet I still loved him and pride stopped me from going back to my parents. But things got worse. All sorts of villains started calling round. Then one day Mother phoned and said my father had died. I went back for the funeral. Hugh asked me if he had left me anything and I said no, truthfully. He had left everything to my mother. Mother sold the farm and moved into a little house in Oban. She was never the same after my father's death. She got cancer and a year later, she was dead, too. She left everything to me. Hugh hadn't come up with me. I saw the lawyers and got the money she'd left and said that any other money from the sale of the house was to go into an account in Oban in my name. But I meant to tell Hugh about the money. I was always hoping he would reform."

A dry sob escaped her. "I went back to Glasgow. He was entertaining his friends. There were bottles everywhere. Hugh had a raddled woman sitting on his knee. I cracked. I said I was leaving him. He turned ugly. He got everyone out and then he beat me with his belt.

I'd brought back some family photos and he threw them on the fire. He said I couldn't leave him. He'd always find me. Then the police broke in during the night and arrested him for armed robbery. I stayed only as long as the trial, only as long as it took to learn he was going to prison, and then I left for Oban. I stayed until my mother's house was sold and then came up here. I decided that people were no good. I'd stick to my croft and my sheep. That Mrs. Dunwiddy was friendly while I was negotiating the sale with her, but she asked too many questions so I never saw her again."

"Mrs. Dunwiddy's down in an old folks home in Inverness. She had a stroke. I believe her mind's gone," said Hamish, not elaborating further because he didn't want the touchy Mrs. Gallagher to know he had been trying to find out about her.

"Oh, dear," she said vaguely.

"So now your worries are over, you should get about and meet people."

"I'm too set in my ways to start socializing, young man. And my worries aren't over. What about my cat?"

"Still searching," said Hamish getting to his feet. He looked down at her helplessly. There was nothing that could be done to combat years of isolation and sourness.

Chapter Four

$\mathcal{H}$amish put in a request to Strathbane for a list of all petty crimes in the Highland area in the past month. Then he decided to go over to Cnothan and make some more inquiries. The day was cold and still. It never snowed on Christmas day but he found himself hoping that just this year there might be a light fall to delight the children. As he passed Mrs. Gallagher's croft, he saw her out in the fields. She seemed to be shouting something. He stopped and switched off the engine and rolled down the window.

"Smoky!" she was calling. "Smoky!"

Her voice echoed round the winter landscape, and the twin mountains above Loch-dubh sent back the wailing echo of her voice. He drove on slowly, looking right and left, suddenly hoping that he would see a grey-and-white cat. But only a startled deer ran across his path and then with one great leap vanished among some stunted trees at the side of the road.

He drove on until he reached Cnothan. He noticed lights had been strung along the main street and two men were erecting a tree in a large tub at the bottom of the street. He called in at Mr. Sinclair's shop. "Oh, it's you," said Mr. Sinclair.

"I see you've got the lights up. Did that mean another collection?"

"No, it did not! I paid for those lights out of my own pocket, so that should shut up those who said I only wanted the lights to make a bit of money."

"No more thefts in Cnothan?"

"Not that I know of. Isn't one theft enough for you?"

"Just wondered. Any news of strangers about the place?"

"Look, I've been too busy with the customers to notice anything."

Hamish looked thoughtfully at him. He wondered if by any mad chance Mr. Sinclair had taken the lights himself and then because of the fuss had handed them back, claiming to have supplied new ones.

He went out of the shop and strolled down towards the loch. He stood for a moment watching the men working on the tree and then he went into the bait shop. Mr. McPhee looked up. "You again."

"Yes, me. I'm still checking around to see if any strangers have been spotted, probably four young men in a four-wheel drive."

"See nothing like that."

Hamish looked around. "You can't do much trade this time of year."

"It's better than sitting at home looking at the telly. I hate Christmas, and that's a fact."

"What will you be doing for Christmas?"

"Sitting getting drunk and trying not to put my foot through the telly. Do you know they're going to show *The Sound of Music* again? It's enough to drive a man mad."

"I tell you what, me and the schoolteacher from Lochbudh are going down on Christmas day to a concert at an old folks home to try and brighten the folks up. Why don't you come with us?"

"I'm not that old. I'm only sixty-eight."

"I'm not old either. But it would be a bit o' fun."

Mr. McPhee peered at him and then said, "Aye, it might be fun. What time would ye be leaving?"

"I'll let you know. Wait a bit. I'll let you know now." Hamish took out his mobile phone. He phoned the Underwoods' number. Bella answered. "What time's the concert to be held, Bella?"

"Three in the afternoon, Hamish. We went to see that Mr. Wilson and he seemed awfully pleased at the idea."

"I'll be there myself with some friends."

"Good. See you then."

Hamish rang off. "I'll pick you up at two o'clock."

Mr. McPhee looked quite animated. "Dearie me," he said, shaking his head. "I don't know when I last had an outing since the wife died."

"When did she die?"

"Two years ago." Bleak loneliness stared out of his eyes. For some reason, Hamish found himself thinking again about Mrs. Gallagher. What a miserable lonely life she led!

"That's fine," he said to Mr. McPhee. "I'll see you Christmas day."

He asked various locals about the village if they had seen any youths about and then drove home to the police station. There was a fax waiting for him from Strathbane. He studied the list of petty thefts. They seemed to be spread all over the place. He studied the list again closely. Any youths who would take lights and a Christmas tree were not experienced thieves. They probably roamed around picking up stuff that was easy to lift. His eyes settled on the thefts in the Lairg area. A crofter had had a toolbox taken from a shed, another, a generator, a third, a supply of cut planks with which he had intended to build a henhouse.

He would take a drive over to Lairg in the morning.

Maisie Pease was on the phone with a friend in Inverness. "I'm telling you, Lucy," she said with a giggle, "I never thought I would end up with the village policeman. Yes, he's quite good-looking. We're going down to some old folks home on Christmas day for a concert, just the two of us, and then I'll make him Christmas dinner, and then who knows what will happen!"

Hamish went along to the general store to buy some groceries early next morning. As he was paying for them, he asked Mr. Patel, "Do you get many of the schoolchildren pinching stuff?"

"Not so many," said the Indian shopkeeper, his white teeth gleaming in his brown face. "I've got these mirrors up, so I usually catch them. Och, it's nothing for you to go worrying about, Hamish. I deal with it myself."

"Know a wee lassie called Morag Anderson?"

"Aye, I ken them all."

"She ever take anything?"

"Come on, Hamish, that lassie's a saint. Always polite. Beautiful manners."

Hamish took his bag of groceries.

"Does the shopping for her parents, does she?"

"No, her mother does that."

"Just buys sweets?"

"Never. She says she isn't allowed sweets."

"No Christmas, no sweets. What a life! What does she buy?"

"Just some cat food."

Hamish froze. It couldn't be, could it?

"Hamish," chided Mr. Patel, "there's a queue behind ye."

"Sorry." Hamish left and stood outside the shop.

"What's up with you, Constable?" demanded a voice. "Standing there like a great loon. Shouldn't you be about your duties?"

Hamish found himself confronted by the

Currie sisters, Nessie and Jessie, twins and spinsters of the parish. They both wore tightly buttoned tweed coats and woolly hats over rigidly permed hair. "What are you standing there gawking at, gawking at?" said Jessie who had an irritating way of repeating everything.

Hamish suddenly smiled blindingly down at them. "At your beauty, ladies."

"Get along with you," said Nessie. "It's not our beauty you're after but that new school-teacher."

"She should be warned, she should be warned," said Jessie.

"Have the Andersons a cat?" asked Hamish.

"What? Them at the big villa at the end?" asked Nessie.

"Yes, them."

"I've never seen one, never seen one," said Jessie. "I shouldn't think so. Herself is verra houseproud, verra houseproud."

"Just wondered," said Hamish, ambling off. He went to the police station and stacked away his groceries.

Now let's go for a mad leap of the imagination, he thought. The saintly Morag steals Mrs. Gallagher's cat. How can she hide it from her parents? Well, her mother had bragged about her having her own separate apartment at the top of the house.

So I could just go along and ask Mrs. Anderson if she has a cat. If she says no, ask her why Morag is buying cat food. I suddenly wish I didn't have to do this. I suddenly wish it was someone else.

He hoped he was wrong. The thought of telling Mrs. Gallagher made him quail. He had no doubt she would press charges. His heart was heavy as he left the police station and walked along the waterfront. He had a weak hope they might not be at home. But the factory at Strathbane would be closed for Christmas and no doubt Mr. Anderson would be at home, just as he had been when Hamish first called.

He rang the bell. Mr. Anderson answered the door. He drew down his brows in a scowl. "If you've come here again to lecture us about Christmas, I'll report you to headquarters."

"I would like to speak to you and your wife. It's a case of theft."

Mr. Anderson looked taken aback. "You'd better come in."

Hamish walked into the dark sitting room where Mrs. Anderson was knitting. She looked up, startled, and a steel knitting needle fell to the floor.

"This officer is here to talk about a theft," said Mr. Anderson, "although what it's got to do with us is beyond me."

"May I sit down?" Hamish took off his cap and sat down before they could say anything. "It's like this," he said. "Mrs. Gallagher who lives out on the Cnothan road, her cat's disappeared."

Mrs. Anderson goggled at him. "What on earth has that got to do with us?"

"Have you got a cat?"

"No, we haven't got a cat!" raged Mr. Anderson. "How dare you come here and imply —"

"Then why is Morag buying cat food?" said Hamish in a flat voice.

They both stared at him.

Then Mr. Anderson went to the foot of the stairs and shouted up, "Morag! Come down here!"

They waited in silence until Morag came in, small and neat in a crisp white blouse and block-pleated skirt.

"This officer says you have been buying cat food," said her father.

Morag turned pale. "I was buying it for someone."

"Who?" asked Hamish gently. "I shall check with the person you say you are buying the cat food for."

Huge tears filled Morag's eyes and she began to sob. The atmosphere in the room was electric.

———

Mrs. Anderson left the room and went upstairs. Morag stood sobbing.

"Will ye no sit down, lassie?" suggested Hamish.

But she continued to cry. Hamish glared at her father. Couldn't he do something or say something?

Mrs. Anderson came back, a smile on her face. "Och, there's no cat up there," she said triumphantly. "All you've done is give Morag a fright."

"It still doesn't explain the cat food," said Hamish. "Mind if I have a look?"

"Oh, go on!" shouted Mrs. Anderson. "But a complaint about you goes straight to Strathbane today. Terrorizing children! You're a monster."

Hamish went up the thickly carpeted stairs. He went into Morag's bedroom. It was white and clean; white bedspread, white flounced curtains. He searched around and under the bed. Then he tried the sitting room and the bathroom without success. There was a door on the landing. He pushed it open. It was a box room full of discarded old furniture and old suitcases. Over by the window, he saw a bowl of water and a bowl of catfood.

"Smoky!" he called.

A faint meow came from one of the suitcases. He noticed it had airholes bored in the sides. He lifted the lid and a small grey-and-white cat blinked up at him. "Come here," he said in a soft voice. He picked up the cat, which snuggled under his chin, and went slowly downstairs.

Mrs. Anderson screamed when she saw him with the cat and Mr. Anderson began to shout and rave at his daughter. She was a limb of Satan. How could she do this after all they had done for her?

"I wanted something to love that would love me back," said Morag, now past crying.

"Did you go into Mrs. Gallagher's house and take the cat?" asked Hamish.

"No," she said, her voice little above a whisper. "I was walking up by her croft after school and I saw the cat. It came up to me. It likes me. Smoky *loves* me. I thought I would take Smoky home and play with him for a bit. That's all. Then I was frightened to take him back."

Hamish turned to the parents. "Look here. No harm done. I've got the cat. Why don't I just tell Mrs. Gallagher I found it wandering by the road? You don't want charges against Morag."

"There will be no lying!" thundered Mr. Anderson. "You will take Morag and that animal to Mrs. Gallagher. It is up to her to punish the girl."

Hamish looked at him in disgust. "Aye, I'll do that and then I'll be back to have a word with you. Get your coat, Morag, and put a scarf on. It's cold out."

He walked with the now silent Morag along the waterfront to where the police Land Rover was parked outside the station. "I want you to take Smoky and hold him on your lap, tight," he ordered. "Cats are sometimes scared if they're not used to motors."

Morag gently took the cat from him and climbed into the passenger seat. In a bleak little voice, she asked, "Will I go to hell?"

"Och, no," said Hamish, letting in the clutch. "Don't you have the telly?"

She shook her head miserably.

"Well, it was on the news. Hell's been abolished. Fact. Trust me. You read your Bible, don't you?"

A nod.

"I mean the New Testament?"

Nod, again.

"Don't ye know the bit about there being more rejoicing in heaven over the entrance of one sinner than that of an honest man, or something like that?"

Her wide eyes looked up at him, startled.

"I am the law," said Hamish grandly, "and I wouldnae lie tae ye."

When they got to Mrs. Gallagher's croft, he said, "Give me the cat and wait there. No running away."

Cradling Smoky against his chest, he knocked at the door. Only one lock clicked and the door was opened.

"Oh, God, it's Smoky," said Mrs. Gallagher. Tears of relief coursed down her face. Hamish was beginning to feel like Alice in the pool of tears.

"I want to talk to you about it," said Hamish, following her in.

She looked at him sharply. "Smoky hasn't been wandering the fields. He's well fed and clean."

"Aye. Let me tell you the story."

He sat down and told her all about Morag, about her strict parents, about how she seemed to have every material comfort but nothing in the way of love. "She said she only wanted something to love that would love her back. Wait!" He held up his hand, seeing the anger on Mrs. Gallagher's face. "I was going to lie to you. It's bad enough you bitching to grownups, but I didn't want you taking your spite out on a wee girl. I wanted to tell you I had just found Smoky wandering about, but those parents from hell made me bring the girl up here, and you can press charges if you want and give the poor bairn a criminal record."

"She's outside?"

"Yes."

"Bring her in."

"All right," said Hamish wearily. "What a Christmas!"

He went out to the Land Rover and said to Morag, "You'd best come in and apologize."

Morag climbed down and then stood looking up at him, her eyes wide with fright. "She's a witch. Everyone says so."

"She's only something that rhymes with it. Witches were abolished in the eighteenth century. I am the law and that is the fact, so stop having these stupid ideas."

They went into the croft house, Hamish gently nudging Morag in front of him.

Morag stood before Mrs. Gallagher. "I am so very sorry," she whispered.

Mrs. Gallagher looked at Hamish. "Get out of here, Officer, and let me have a word with the girl." Hamish hesitated. "Go on. I'm not going to eat her."

Hamish reluctantly went outside and got into the Land Rover. He had given up smoking some years ago and now he was glad there were no shops nearby. He had a sudden sharp craving for a cigarette. He waited and waited. At last he could bear it no longer. He went back to the croft house and walked in.

Mrs. Gallagher and Morag were sitting in front of the television set. Morag had Smoky on her lap. Mrs. Gallagher stood up and said to Hamish, "A word with you outside."

Hamish walked out with her, and Mrs. Gallagher turned to him. "You can go back to her parents and tell her that Morag's punishment is that she's to come up here every afternoon during the school holidays. Tell them it's a community service."

Hamish grinned and bent down and kissed her on the cheek. "I'll pick her up at five o'clock," he said. He marched off to the Land Rover.

Hamish drove off whistling. Now for those parents.

When he followed Mr. Anderson into the sitting room, the angry words he had rehearsed died on his lips. Mrs. Anderson had been crying. Her eyes were red and swollen. More tears, thought Hamish. What a day for tears!

"It has turned out all right," he said evenly, "but no thanks to you. Mrs. Gallagher wants Morag to go to her every afternoon during the holidays as a sort of community service. Morag is with her at the moment and will be home at five. Now, she was wrong to take the cat, but it seems to be that a lassie with no friends and grim parents needed something to love."

"But we do love her. We give her everything!" cried Mrs. Anderson.

"Aye, she's got her own wee flat where nobody ever comes. She sees the other children getting excited about Santa Claus and knows there is no Christmas for her, no fun. Now I know your minister and he's a good man, and I don't think he would like you to be torturing a wee girl by forbidding Christmas. She does well at school and I bet you take it for granted. I bet you think that because she's got her own flat, she owes you. There's more to life than material things. To try to get your child sentenced in a criminal court over a damn cat is beyond my comprehension. You could have ruined her life. You had her when you were both on in years, so she doesn't have young parents to take her on picnics or to the movies."

"The movies are the work of the devil," said Mr. Anderson heavily. "Naked lewd women—"

"Aw, shut your face, you dirty auld man!" Hamish shouted, losing his temper completely. "Haff you neffer heard o' Walt Disney? You go on banning everything in her life that's fun and she'll run away from ye as soon as she's old enough. I've seen it happen time and again. And parents like you sit there and wonder why and neffer look at their own behavior. If you're thinking of reporting me to Strathbane, forget it. I'll deny everything about that cat and so, if I'm not mistaken, will Mrs. Gallagher. Oh, for God's sake, lighten up. This place is like a morgue. I'm going now, but I'll be checking on ye. And if you persecute Morag over this, I'll have the Royal Society for the Protection of Children on your doorstep. Good day to you."

He marched off. As he drove to the police station, he said, "Movies the work o' the devil! Havers!"

"Have you ever seen *Star Wars*?" Mrs. Gallagher asked Morag.

"No, Mrs. Gallagher."

"Call me Alice. It so happens I have a video here."

Mrs. Gallagher put the tape in the video machine and sat back with a sigh of pleasure. It was nice to have someone to watch things with. She didn't need to worry about Morag gossiping or being cruel. She was just a little girl. Not like a grownup. But grand company for all that.

Hamish went back at five o'clock to pick up

Morag. She waved goodbye to Mrs. Gallagher and shouted, "See you tomorrow, Alice!"

"So it's Alice, is it?" asked Hamish.

"I had a grand time," said Morag.

"Well, she needs the company."

The happy look left her face. "My parents are going to be mad at me."

"It sometimes doesn't do to let people know the whole truth," said Hamish cautiously. "What did you do this afternoon?"

"We watched *Star Wars*."

"Aye, well, I would keep quiet about that. Just say you're keeping the old lady company, helping about the croft."

"Dad doesn't approve of the movies."

"No, he doesn't. So go easy. You've got off lightly."

He went into the house with her. "Afore I go," he said sternly to Morag's parents. "We could get round this Christmas business and ye could be helping with a bit o' Christian work. There's a concert for the old folks down in Inverness on Christmas day. I'm taking Miss Pease, the schoolteacher, and Mrs. Gallagher and Morag, I am sure, would like to come. It would cheer the old folks up to see a girl like Morag. She seems to have a way with old people. And she would be doing her Christian duty."

He waited for a rant of protest, but Mr. Anderson said wearily, "I can see nothing against that."

"Right, I'll drive you all down. And I think Morag's been punished enough. Mrs. Gallagher will be down to pick her up at noon tomorrow."

Hamish made his escape. He'd better rent that bus from the garage. They'd never all fit into the police Land Rover.

Maisie was studying a cherry red dress. It looked nice and festive and would do for Christmas day. She dreamily pictured the long drive down to Inverness with Hamish. In her mind, he put his hand on her knee and said, "I've been thinking of settling down." Ah, well, when you got a man on his own, there was no saying what could happen.

The next day Hamish, realizing all the business about Morag had delayed his visit to Lairg, drove over there to see if he could find out anything. The day was even colder than the one before, with a steel-blue sky above and un-melted frost sparkling on the trees and grass.

He dropped into various shops on the main street until in the butcher's, a woman heard him questioning the butcher and turned round and said, "There were a couple of lads trying to flog boxes of Christmas lights."

Hamish took out his notebook. "Can you give me a description?"

"One o' them had dyed blonde hair and one o' thae rings through his nose. T'other was squat and dark. The fair one was wearing a red anorak and jeans and the dark one, an old tweed coat and jeans as well."

"What were they wearing on their feet?"

"We used to call them 'sandshoes,' then they were called 'sneakers,' now they're called 'running shoes.' Them white things."

"Thanks. Any other distinguishing marks? Tattoos? Funny haircuts?"

"They were wrapped up so I don't know about tattoos. What d'you mean, funny haircuts?"

"Spikes or shaved all over or something like that?"

"The dark one was going a bit bald. That's all."

Hamish went out of the shop and worked his way down the street, stopping to talk to the locals, asking questions, until one man volunteered that he had seen two men answering the description Hamish had given, getting into a small truck. No, he hadn't noticed the registration, but it was old and muddy and painted blue.

Hamish decided to search outside Lairg. He

dropped in at the croft houses at Rhianbrech outside Lairg but no one there had seen anything, then past the station, always looking right and left. Then he went back through Lairg and out on the Lochinver road, cursing the rapidly failing light.

His eyes were getting weary with straining into the surrounding wilderness and he was tired of driving along at ten miles an hour. He decided to put his foot down and go on into Lochinver for a cup of tea. Then he saw a glimmer of white across the moorland. He stopped abruptly and climbed out of the Land Rover. In the gloaming, he could just make out a white trailer. He set out across the moorland. The sun had gone down and great stars were beginning to twinkle against a greenish sky.

As he approached, he saw the blue-painted tailgate of a truck parked beside the trailer. There was a dim light shining through the curtained windows. Hamish did not feel like tackling two, possibly four, young men on his own. If I were in a film, he thought, I would render them all helpless with a few well-placed karate chops. But this wasn't a film, yet he was reluctant to phone for backup unless he had some proof.

He silently crept up. The back of the truck was covered with a tarpaulin. He looked underneath it and in the fading light saw boxes and boxes of Christmas lights. On the other side of the truck, he found a Christmas tree lying on its side.

He quickly and quietly sprinted back to the Land Rover and phoned headquarters at Strathbane. "I'll go on into Lochinver," he said after he had given his report. "I don't want one of them looking out of the window and seeing a police vehicle."

He set off for Lochinver and parked by the waterfront and waited, cursing the long distances in the Highlands. He hoped the police contingent wouldn't come racing along the Lochinver road with lights flashing and sirens blaring.

At last four police cars arrived and Hamish's heart sank when Detective Chief Inspector Blair heaved his bulk out of the leading car.

"I would have thought this would have been too small a case for you, sir," said Hamish.

"I think these are the lads responsible for a chain o' thefts across Sutherland," said Blair. "Just tell us where they are, laddie, and get back to yer sheep."

Hamish stood his ground. "It's dark and you won't find them without me."

"Oh, all right. Lead the way."

Hamish drove off and the police cars fell in

behind him. Curtains twitched in cottage windows. He found himself hoping that none of them had a girlfriend in Lochinver. In these days of mobile phones, villains could be communicated with just when you didn't want them to be.

He pulled up down the road and peered across the moorland. The trailer was still there. He hoped they were all inside. He got out and set off without waiting for Blair and the others. But he knew they would be quickly behind him. Blair was not going to let Hamish Macbeth take any credit for this.

When he reached the trailer, Blair's truculent voice whispered in the darkness. "All right, Macbeth, knock on the door and then leave the rest tae us."

Hamish knocked on the door. "Who is it?" called a voice from inside.

"Police!"

Then loud and clear he heard a dog give a warning bark. He knew that bark. It was his dead dog, Towser. He threw himself on the ground to the side of the door just as a shotgun blast shattered the door and would have shattered one Highland policeman had he been standing in front of it.

"You're surrounded!" he yelled, getting to his feet. "And we're armed. Throw out that gun and come out with your hands in the air."

There was silence from the trailer. Hamish cursed. He had never thought for a moment that they would be armed.

The door was kicked open and the men emerged, one by one, their hands on their heads. Blair took over and ordered them to lie on the ground, where they were handcuffed. The charges were announced: theft and attempted murder of a police officer. The men were led off to a police car.

"You're a fool," Blair snapped at Hamish. "Putting our lives at risk by failing to tell us they were armed."

"I didn't know and you didn't know," protested Hamish. "And it was me that was nearly killed."

"But you knew that shot was coming. How?"

Hamish grinned. "Highland intuition."

"Crap," muttered Blair.

After they had gone, Hamish found his hands were trembling. He drove back into Lochinver and went into a hotel bar and ordered a double whisky. Then he ordered a pot of coffee. The germ of an idea was forming in his brain. He waited for a couple of hours and then set out for the trailer again. A forensic team was just packing up.

"That truck with all the lights in it shouldn't be left there," said Hamish. "Someone might pinch them. Are the keys to the truck around?"

"They were in the ignition."

"Right, maybe it would be a good idea if one of you could drive the truck to the police station where I can take care of them."

"I suppose we could do that." One of them said, "You two, go with this officer and take that truck and leave it at Lochdubh police station. It is Macbeth, isn't it?"

"Aye."

"I've heard of you."

"Wait a bit. Could you take the tree as well?"

"Come on. Who's going to take a big tree like that?"

"You never know."

"Okay. Boys, put that tree on the back of the truck."

After the lights had been stacked in the police office and the tree stacked at the back of the police station, Hamish said goodbye to the two forensic men. He then made himself a meal and went to bed. Tomorrow was Christmas Eve and he had just had an outrageous idea. But he would need help.

In the morning Hamish went along to the

local garage to see the owner, Ian Chisholm. "I want to hire that Volkswagen minibus of yours," he said. "I'm taking some folks down to Inverness on Christmas day. Is it still working?"

"Good as new. Come and see."

He led the way through to the yard at the back. The old minibus stood in all its horrible red-and-yellow glory, Ian having run out of red paint and gone on to yellow. His wife had made chintz covers for the passenger seats and it looked, as Hamish thought, as daft a conveyance as ever.

"I'll take it," he said.

He made his way back to the police station and saw the small figure of Morag running towards him. "Glad to see you," said Hamish. "Tell your parents and Mrs. Gallagher that we'll be leaving at one-thirty from the war memorial on the waterfront. What's up? You look a wee bit strained. Parents been giving you a hard time?"

"No, they say Mrs. Gallagher's punishment enough. It's not that."

"So what is it?"

"Mrs. Gallagher's a Roman Catholic."

Hamish privately cursed all religious bigotry everywhere. If the Andersons knew that Mrs. Gallagher was a Catholic, their precious child would not be allowed anywhere near her.

He forced his voice to sound casual and not reflect the rage and frustration he felt.

"I would not be bothering them with such a thing at Christmas. Sometimes it is better not to trouble people with facts that would distress them."

"So it's all right not to tell?"

"Oh, yes."

And God forgive me for encouraging a wee lassie to lie to her parents, thought Hamish as Morag scampered off. Then he quietened his conscience by reflecting that he hadn't exactly told her to lie, he had just advised her not to say anything.

He walked on. As he passed Patel's, none other than Mrs. Gallagher emerged. She had two carrier bags and Hamish could see they were full of Christmas decorations. "That's nice," he said, indicating the bags. "Getting ready for Christmas?"

"Why don't you mind your own business?" demanded Mrs. Gallagher. "Haven't you got any work to do?"

"I've told Morag I'm picking you up at the waterfront at one-thirty tomorrow. Chust make sure you don't die o' spleen afore then," snapped Hamish.

She glared at him and then the anger died

out of her face and she let out a surprisingly girlish giggle. She was still giggling as she walked to her car.

"Whit's up wi' that old crone?" asked a voice at his elbow. Hamish looked down and saw Archie Maclean. "I havenae seen that woman laugh afore," remarked Archie. "Whit happened? Did she see someone slip on a banana skin and break a leg?"

"Never mind her. I need some help, Archie. Come into the police station and have a dram."

Archie's face brightened. "Grand. But don't be telling the wife."

In the police station, Hamish poured two glasses of whisky. "Listen to me, Archie, I need you and some of the more liberal-minded fisherman to help me."

Chapter Five

*T*hat afternoon, a group of children met outside Patel's to share sweets and talk about what they hoped to get from Santa Claus. A red-haired little boy called Sean Morrison said, "Folks say Morag has been visiting Mrs. Gallagher."

There was an amazed chorus, "That old witch! Maybe she'll put a spell on her."

Then Kirsty Taylor, a blonde who already had a flirtatious eye heralding trouble to come, said, "I bet you, Sean, you wouldn't have the guts to go out there and ask for Morag."

"Bet you I could."

"Bet you can't."

"I'll go if you all come wi' me," said Sean.

Kirsty danced around him, singing, "Cowardy, cowardy custard."

"If you don't come," shouted Sean, "you won't know I've been there!"

So it was decided they would all go. Sean would knock at the door and they would hide.

"Who can that be?" asked Mrs. Gallagher as she heard the knock at the door.

"I'll go if you like," said Morag.

"No, it's all right." Mrs. Gallagher opened the door and looked down at the trembling figure of Sean. "Is Morag here?" he asked.

"Come in," said Mrs. Gallagher.

"He hasnae come out," whispered Kirsty. "Maybe she's putting them both in the pot to boil them for her supper. I'll creep up and peek in the window."

The others clutched one another as Kirsty crept up to the window. At last she came running back, blonde hair flying, cheeks red in the frosty air. "They're sitting at the fire eating fruitcake," she gasped. "Fruitcake with icing on top."

Mrs. Gallagher opened the door and saw the group of schoolchildren, all professing to be friends of Morag. Mrs. Gallagher knew from Morag that the girl craved friends and was shrewd enough to know why this lot had come round. She knew her local reputation.

"Come in," she said. "There's plenty of cake and lemonade. But first, you've got to give me your phone numbers and I'll phone your parents and let them know where you are." She wrote down the phone numbers and names and went to the phone in her parlour. When she returned to the kitchen, Morag was surrounded by chattering children.

"I'll give you all some cake," said Mrs. Gallagher, "and then you can all help me to put up the Christmas decorations. I'm a bit late this year."

When had she last put up decorations? she wondered, looking back down the years. She cut generous slices of fruitcake while Smoky purred on Morag's lap.

Hamish phoned Maisie Pease. "I'll be setting off from the war memorial tomorrow," he said. "Pick you up at one-thirty."

"Grand, Hamish, I'll see you there."

She rang off and then stared at the phone. How odd? Why wasn't he picking her up at the schoolhouse? She looked through to her neat kitchen where a large turkey lay waiting to be roasted. She had bought a large one to make it look really Christmassy in a Dickensian way. It was too large, she thought. She would be eating turkey for a month.

Jessie and Nessie Currie set out arm in arm for their usual tour of the village. They liked to keep an eye on everything that was going on. As they passed Chisholm's garage, Ian was hosing down the minibus.

"It'll freeze in this weather," said Nessie.

"Freeze in this weather," echoed the Greek chorus that was her twin sister.

"Just getting it ready for Macbeth," said Ian.

"And why would he want a bus?" asked Nessie.

"Don't know. But he's booked it for Christmas day."

The sisters headed for the police station, eyes gleaming with curiosity. Then Nessie grabbed her sister's arm. "Look at that!"

Angela Brodie was pushing a pram along the waterfront. "Herself is past having the babies," exclaimed Nessie.

"Herself has never been able to have the babies, the babies," said Jessie.

They crossed the road and stood in front of Angela. "Who does the little one belong to?" asked Nessie.

"Me!" said Angela with a smile, and pushing the pram around them, headed for home.

"It is the fertility treatment," said Nessie.

They went to the kitchen door of the police station. Jessie peered round Hamish's tall figure. The kitchen seemed to be full of fishermen.

"What's going on, what's going on?" asked Jessie.

"Crime prevention meeting," said Hamish curtly. "What can I do for you?"

"You hired a bus for the morrow," said Nessie. "Why?"

"I'm taking some people down to an old folks home in Inverness for a Christmas Day concert."

The sisters looked at each other. Then they said in unison. "We'll come."

Hamish wanted to be rid of them. "All right," he said. "The bus leaves the war memorial at one-thirty."

"We'll be there."

I don't want them, thought Hamish, but if that pair is determined to come, there'll be no stopping them.

At two in the morning on Christmas day, there was a wickedly hard frost, which turned the whole landscape white. Silently and quickly Hamish and the fishermen set to work. Archie paused in his labours to whisper to

105

Hamish, "What will you say if Strathbane finds you out?"

"I'll say I'm testing them," Hamish whispered back. "To see if they work. It's the one day only."

Christmas day. Morag struggled awake and switched on her bedside light. She knew she should not hope that Santa had brought her anything, but she wistfully thought it would be wonderful if just this year he had decided to stop at her home.

She climbed out of bed and drew back the curtains. Then she let out a gasp. It was snowing, large feathery flakes falling down from a black sky.

But not only that. She rubbed her eyes and looked again. The Anderson house was at an angle so that the windows faced down the waterfront. Fairy lights were winking and sparkling through the snow, and by the memorial was a large Christmas tree, also bedecked in lights.

She hurriedly washed and dressed and was about to rush from her room when she saw a bulging stocking hanging on the end of her bed. Wondering, she tipped out the contents. There was a giant bar of chocolate, a small racing car, nuts and oranges. Santa must have come. Her parents would never have allowed her chocolate.

She went into the sitting room. Four packages wrapped in Christmas paper stood on the coffee table. Eagerly, she opened them up. Three labels said TO MORAG FROM HER MOTHER AND FATHER. In one package was a smoky blue Shetland scarf, in another, a bright red sweater, and in the third, a doll with blonde hair and blue eyes. The fourth package was from Mrs. Gallagher and contained a handsome wooden box of tubes of watercolors and brushes, and along with it came a large drawing book.

She was about to run and find her parents, when she distinctly heard sleigh bells outside and a great voice crying, "Ho, ho, ho!"

"Santa!" Morag ran to the front door and jerked it open. The snow fell gently and the lights of a transformed Lochdubh glittered and sent their reflections across the black loch. She looked up at the sky but there was no fleeing sleigh. Then she saw the parcel lying on the doorstep. The label said TO MORAG FROM SANTA WITH LOVE.

She carried it into the sitting room and squatted down on the floor with the parcel on her lap and opened it up. It was a large stuffed grey-and-white cat, like Smoky, with green glass eyes.

Morag ran up to her parents' bedroom and threw open the door. Her parents struggled awake as the small figure of their daughter hurled herself on the bed, hugging them and kissing them and saying, "It's wonderful! I've never been so happy in all my life!"

And Mr. Anderson, who had been prepared to break the news to his daughter that there was no such person as Santa Claus, followed by his usual lecture on the pagan flummery of Christmas, found his eyes filling with tears as he hugged his daughter back and merely said gruffly, "Glad you're happy."

In the police station, Hamish Macbeth put the tape recorder with the sound of sleigh bells and "Santa's" voice along with the chain of small gilt bells he had borrowed from Angela on the kitchen table. Time to get a few hours' sleep before the journey to Inverness.

In the cottage next to the schoolhouse, Maisie Pease had a leisurely bath, and then began to dress with care, first in satin underwear and then in the cherry-red wool dress. She looked thoughtfully at the large sprig of mistletoe hanging over the living room door. She would point at it shyly and he would gather her in his arms. "You're looking bonnie," he would say before his lips descended on hers. She gave a happy little sigh and went to look out of the window. Where had all the lights come from? They sparkled the length of the waterfront. The snow was falling gently and she hoped it would not thicken and stop them from going.

She tried to eat breakfast, but excitement had taken her appetite away. How slow the hands of the clock moved. She waited and waited as the sky reluctantly lightened outside. She looked out of the window again. The snow had stopped and a little red winter sun was struggling over the horizon. Ten o'clock in the morning. Three hours to wait. Maisie switched on the television set and prayed for time to speed up.

Angela Brodie opened the door to the Currie sisters. "Happy Christmas!" cried Angela. "Come in and have a glass of sherry."

The sisters came in and sat down in Angela's messy kitchen. Nessie handed Angela two small parcels. "For the baby," she said.

Angela looked at them in amazement. "What baby?"

"Yours. The one you were pushing in the pram."

Angela blushed with embarrassment. "I'm sorry. I never thought for a moment you would believe me. It was a cloutie dumpling. I'd been using Mrs. Maclean's washhouse. I'm sorry I've put you to expense. Let me pay you."

"That will not be necessary, not necessary," said Jessie. "We'll just put them away. Someone's always having a baby, a baby."

"Sherry?"

"No," said Nessie, "we're going down to Inverness with Macbeth. He's taking us in Chisholm's bus. It's a concert he's organised at an old folks home."

"What a surprising man he is. Can anyone come? We're not having dinner until this evening."

"The bus leaves the war memorial at one-thirty."

"I'll see if my husband wants to come and maybe join you."

Maisie Pease stared at the carnival-painted bus and then walked round it, looking for the police Land Rover. On the other side, she found Hamish with a group of people.

"Maisie!" he cried. "Are we all set?"

"Yes," she said eagerly.

"Right, I think that's everyone," said Hamish. "All on the bus."

Maisie watched in dismay as the Currie sisters, Dr. Brodie and his wife, Angela, Mr. and

Mrs. Anderson, Morag and Mrs. Gallagher all climbed aboard. Hamish was at the wheel. There would be no chance for any intimate talk.

Then she brightened up. They would be alone for dinner that evening.

Despite the odd assortment of villagers, there was a festive air on the bus. Angela laughed at the chintz-covered seats. The bus sped out of Lochdubh under a now sunny sky. Snow lay in a gentle blanket everywhere. It was a magic landscape, thought Morag, clutching the stuffed cat on her lap as she sat next to Mrs. Gallagher.

They stopped in Cnothan and picked up Mr. McPhee. Maisie groaned inwardly. How many more?

The Currie sisters were flirting awfully with Mr. McPhee, whose old face was beginning to assume a hunted look.

He moved his seat to the back of the bus. Thwarted, the Currie sisters began to sing carols in high, reedy, churchy voices. Hamish was amused this time to hear Jessie repeating the last line of every lyric and falling behind her sister.

When they were finally silent, Hamish, his eyes twinkling with mischief, called to Mr. Anderson to give them a song. To his surprise he began to sing "The Road to the Isles" in a clear tenor. Morag sparkled when her father finished and was given a round of applause.

At last Hamish drew up outside the old folks home and they all climbed down.

A piano had been set up in the lounge. Residents of the home sat around. Bella and Charlie were already at the piano dressed in striped blazers and straw boaters.

Mrs. Dunwiddy exclaimed, "Is it really you, Alice?"

"One of her good days," Mrs. Kirk whispered to Hamish.

They all sat down and were served with sweet sherry and slices of Christmas cake. The lights were switched off except for a light over the piano and the glittering lights on the tree.

Bella and Charlie were really good, thought Hamish as they belted out all the old songs, Charlie playing and both singing, their voices still full and strong. Elderly faces beamed, arthritic fingers tapping out the rhythm on the arms of chairs.

Morag sat clutching her father's hand and thought her heart would burst with happiness. In that moment, she decided that she would be a policewoman when she grew up and be as much like Hamish Macbeth as possible.

Only Maisie felt let down. It was not that

Hamish was ignoring her. It was just that he treated her with the same friendliness as the rest of the party. She thought of the large turkey that she had cooked the night before so that it only needed to be heated. Would Hamish think it excessive? There had been a television program on world famine, and then thinking of those stick-like people and the sheer waste of that overlarge bird, Maisie felt guilty.

The concert finished at five and then after more sherry and cake, they all climbed back on the bus.

As Hamish drove out of Inverness on the A-9, it began to snow again, great gusts of white whipping across his vision.

He wondered what on earth he would do with this busload if he got stuck. He called back to Mr. McPhee, "Would you mind if I went straight to Lochdubh? I can put you up for the night." He remembered Maisie's dinner and said over his shoulder, "Is that all right with you, Maisie?"

"Oh, sure," said Maisie, sarcastic with bitter disappointment. "Why not bring everyone?"

Hamish missed the sarcasm in her voice and said warmly, "That's really good of you."

"Yes, it is," said Angela. "I'll drop off at our place and pick up the turkey and dumpling. Everything's ready. We'll have a feast."

"If we ever get there," said Hamish.

Morag crept down the bus and clutched her father's arm. "Daddy, can we go, too?"

He looked down into her wide pleading eyes and bit back the angry refusal. "Well, just this once."

And it will be just this once, thought Maisie angrily. She thought of the boyfriend down in Inverness that she had jilted. She had been cruel. She would phone him up and make amends.

Hamish was often to wonder afterwards how he had ever managed to drive that bus to Lochdubh or how the old vehicle had managed to plough up and down the hills as the storm increased in force. He let out a slow sigh of relief as they lurched over the humpbacked bridge that led into the village and saw the Christmas lights dancing crazily in the wind.

It was only after Angela and Dr. Brodie had collected their contributions to the meal that Maisie began to brighten up. As the women helped her in the kitchen and the men laid the table and then went out into the storm to make forays to collect more chairs, she was surrounded by so many people thanking her that she began to get a warm glow. Her spirits sank a little as Mr. McPhee grabbed her under the mistletoe and gave her a smacking kiss, but lightened again as soon as everyone was seated round the table in front of large plates of turkey and stuffing, chipolatta sausages, steaming gravy and roast potatoes. Bowls of vegetables were passed from hand to hand. Wine was poured, although the Andersons and Morag stuck to cranberry juice.

Hamish rose to his feet. "A toast to Maisie for the best Christmas ever!"

Everyone raised their glasses. "To Maisie!"

When the turkey was finished and the plates cleared, Angela said brightly, "The dumpling's heating in the oven. I'll get it if some of you ladies will help me with the plates."

Hamish watched nervously as the large brown dumpling was carried in and placed reverently in the middle of the table. Angela's lousy cooking was legendary.

"Would you do the honours, Hamish?" said Angela brightly.

Hamish reluctantly picked up a knife and sank it into the pudding. He cut the first slice and spooned it onto a plate and then filled the other plates. It looked good, but with Angela's cooking, you never could tell until you'd tasted it.

Custard was poured over the slices. Here goes, thought Hamish. He cautiously took a mouthful. It was delicious! What an odd Christmas, he thought. For once in her life, Angela's got it right.

Mrs. Gallagher and Mr. McPhee had discovered a mutual interest in birdwatching and were chatting busily. The Currie sisters who had strict Christian beliefs were talking happily about the iniquities of the world to the Andersons. Morag was telling Angela about her Christmas and Maisie was flushed and happy at the success of her dinner party.

"Who can that be?" demanded Mrs. Wellington, the minister's wife.

"Why don't you answer the phone and find out?" suggested her husband patiently.

Mrs. Wellington picked up the receiver.

"Hullo, Mrs. Wellington, this is Priscilla."

"Merry Christmas. Where are you?"

"In New York."

"Would you believe it? The line's so clear you could be next door. Everything all right?"

"Yes, fine. Look, I've been phoning the police station. I've been trying to get hold of Hamish to wish him a happy Christmas. Do you know where he is?"

"You could try the schoolteacher's place. He might be there."

There was a long silence.

Then Priscilla said, "Have you her number?"

"Wait a minute. I'll look in my book."

"Who's that?" asked the minister.

"It's Priscilla. She wants to talk to Hamish. I'm getting her the schoolteacher's number."

"Maybe you shouldn't have suggested he might be there."

"Oh, why?"

The minister sighed. "You wouldn't understand."

His wife gave him a baffled look and then located the number in her book and picked up the receiver again. "Are you still there? It's Lochdubh six-o-seven-one."

At the schoolhouse the table had been cleared away and a ceilidh had started in the living room, that is, everyone performing something or other. The Currie sisters had taken up positions in front of the fire and were singing in high, shrill voices.

"I'll get some coffee," said Maisie.

"I'll come and help you."

One last try, thought Maisie. She stopped right under the sprig of mistletoe and smiled up at Hamish invitingly. He put his arms about her and smiled back. Maisie tilted back her head and closed her eyes. At that moment, the phone rang loudly and shrilly.

Hamish released her. "You'd better answer that. I'll get the coffee."

Cursing, Maisie picked up the phone.

"Priscilla Halburton-Smythe here," said a voice as cold as the snow outside. "I wish to speak to Hamish Macbeth."

"I'll see if he's here," said Maisie haughtily.

"Who is it?" asked Hamish.

"It's for you." Maisie went back to join the others.

The phone was in the little cottage hall. Hamish picked it up. "Lochdubh Police," he said automatically.

"It's me, Priscilla."

Hamish sank down on the floor, holding the phone.

"It's yourself. How's New York?"

"Oh, you know, very bustling, very energetic as usual. I'm just about to go out to have dinner with friends."

"Bit late, isn't it?"

"I'm five hours behind you, remember?"

"So you are. Merry Christmas. How did you know where to find me?"

"Merry Christmas, Hamish. Mr. Johnston told me you were romancing the schoolteacher and so I assumed you'd be there."

"Why on earth would he say a thing like that? We're just friends."

———

"Just a cosy evening for the two of you?"

"No, there's a lot of people here. I'm just one of the guests. I'll tell you what happened." Hamish told her about the cat and the lights and the visit to the old folks home.

"Sounds like fun," said Priscilla.

"Will you be back for the New Year?"

"No, I'll be here for another six months."

"Now what'll I do if I get the murder case and havenae my Watson?" teased Hamish.

"I'll give you my number. You can always phone me. Write it down, and the address."

"Wait a bit." Hamish found a notepad on a table in the hall with a pen. "Fire away," he said.

She gave him the number and address and then said, "There are a lot of cheap fares to the States nowadays, Hamish. You could always hop on a plane."

"I could always do that," said Hamish happily, forgetting in that moment all about the state of his bank balance.

"Why aren't you over at Rogart with the family?"

Hamish told her about the soap powder competition and Priscilla laughed. "It is good to hear you, Hamish, and it would be good to see you again."

"Aye, well, you never know."

___

They wished each other a merry Christmas again and said goodbye.

Maisie looked up as Hamish came into the room. His face looked as if it were lit up from within. "We were just discussing sleeping arrangements," she said. "It's too bad a night for Mrs. Gallagher to get back home so Mr. and Mrs. Anderson have kindly offered to put her and Mr. McPhee up for the night."

"What about Smoky?" asked Morag anxiously.

"Smoky will be fine," said Mrs. Gallagher. "I've left him plenty of food and water."

So the party broke up. Hamish stood with the others outside the schoolhouse. The snow had stopped and lay white and glistening under the sparkling fairy lights.

Maisie watched them all go and then went indoors to phone the boyfriend she had so cruelly jilted.

Hamish walked along to the police station. He felt very tired. He took out his key but as he bent to unlock the kitchen door, he heard a faint noise from inside. He went to the police Land Rover and took out a hefty spanner to use as a weapon. Then he softly unlocked the door, threw it open and clicked on the kitchen light. A small dog trotted up to him and started sniffing at his trousers. It had a label attached to its collar. He squatted down by the animal and read the label. "To Hamish from Archie. Merry Christmas."

Hamish groaned. The fisherman knew there was a spare key to the police station kept in the gutter above the kitchen door. He must have let himself in with the dog while Hamish had been in Inverness. Hamish didn't want another dog. Once you've broken your heart over one dog, you don't want another. And it was such an odd dog. It was a mongrel, small and rough haired with floppy ears and blue eyes. Hamish could not remember ever having seen a dog with blue eyes. It licked his hand and jumped up to lick his face.

"Have you eaten?" asked Hamish. The dog wagged the stump of its tail energetically.

"I'd better give ye something." Hamish poured a bowl of water and then searched in the cupboards. Then he remembered he had a steak out in the freezer. By the time he had defrosted it, cooked it and chopped it up for the dog, he felt exhausted. He got ready for bed and then fell facedown and drifted off into a dream where he was walking along Fifth Avenue in New York with Priscilla on his arm.

And then the phone rang from the police office. He came awake and sat up. The dog was sitting on the end of the bed looking at him with those odd eyes. He was tempted to let the phone ring and let the answering machine pick up the call, but he remembered the weather and was frightened it might be a report of someone stranded up on the moors.

He went into the police office and picked up the phone. It was Detective Jimmy Anderson from Strathbane. "Is that you, Hamish?" he said. "Well, you'd better move your arse and get thae lights down."

"Why?" asked Hamish, too sleepy to deny anything about the lights.

"There's a man called Sinclair over in Cnothan. Someone told him that Lochdubh was all lit up and he's fuming that they're his lights that the forensic boys said you took to the station. Blair heard about it and he's planning to get over there first thing in the morning."

"He won't manage it," said Hamish. "The roads'll be blocked."

"Hamish, he thinks he's got you this time. He was talking about taking the helicopter. He was drinking all day and I tried to tell him the super would be furious at him for getting a helicopter out, all that expense for some Christmas lights, but he's determined."

"I'll see to it." Hamish dressed hurriedly and then began to phone round the village.

Hamish and his army of fishermen worked all night, taking down the lights, carefully packing them back into the boxes, taking down the Christmas tree and propping it back up against the wall of the police station. Other villagers came out to help. Word flew from house to house that Hamish Macbeth was in trouble and that his superior officer was about to descend from the skies like the wrath of God.

Even Mr. Patel set to work, making sure the lights were all correctly packed so there would be no sign they had ever been taken out of their boxes.

At last the work was finished and everyone crowded into the police station for a celebration party. Mr. Patel presented Hamish with tins of dog food, for Hamish had told him about the dog.

"What are ye going to call him?" asked Archie.

Hamish longed to say that he didn't want another dog, but the dog looked at him and he looked back at the dog and said instead, "I don't know. Where did you find him?"

"I found the poor wee soul wandering up on

the moors," said Archie, "and I thought, that's the very dog for Hamish."

"But Archie, someone may be looking for it."

"Don't think so. It was running up and down the road as if it had been dumped out of a car. Why not call it Frank?"

"Why Frank?"

"You know. Ol' Blue Eyes."

"Frank," said Hamish to the dog.

He turned to Archie. "He doesn't like it."

Another of the fishermen laughed and said, "Look at the lugs on it," referring to the dog's floppy ears.

"What about it?" said Hamish to the dog. "Like the name Lugs?"

The dog wagged its tail and put a paw on Hamish's trouser leg.

They all raised their glasses. "To Lugs!"

"Shh!" said Hamish, holding up a hand for silence. He opened the kitchen door and stepped outside. The sky was turning pale grey. He could hear the sound of an approaching helicopter.

"He's coming, boys!" shouted Hamish.

They scattered out of the police station while Hamish changed into his uniform.

• • •

Blair crouched forward in the helicopter. "Can ye see any lights?" he roared at the pilot.

"Nothing but a few house lights!" the pilot shouted back.

Blair was sobering up rapidly and a little worm of fear began to gnaw his stomach.

"Set down on the front!" he yelled.

The pilot landed next to the Chisholms' bus. Blair climbed down and ducked under the still rotating blades. He glared up and down the waterfront. Not one single Christmas light winked back at him.

He marched to the police station and walked right in. Hamish, neat in his uniform, was sitting at the desk in the police station typing something on the computer.

"Where are those lights?" demanded Blair.

"The Cnothan lights?" said Hamish innocently. "Look about ye, sir. Boxes and boxes of them."

Blair ripped open one of the boxes and glared down at the neatly packed lights. "I'll need to put in a report about that box," said Hamish. "You're destroying the evidence."

"Look, here, Macbeth, I had a report you had thae lights strung up all over the village."

Hamish looked suitably amazed. "Now who would go saying a thing like that?"

Blair stamped out. He went from house to house, demanding to know if anyone had seen any lights, but all shook their heads.

Beside himself with worry and rage, he went back to the police station. Hamish held out the phone. "You're just in time. Superintendent Daviot on the line."

"What the hell are you about taking out the helicopter?" roared Daviot. Blair opened his mouth to lie, to say he had heard of a crack house in Lochdubh, anything, but Daviot was going on. "It's all round Strathbane that you heard Macbeth had put up Christmas lights from that robbery all over his village. Well, did he?"

"There's nothing here, sir. But you see—"

"Listen to this. The pilot will be charging double because it's Christmas and I think the cost should come out of your wages. Return here immediately!"

Blair put down the phone. He walked to the door of the police office. "I'll have you yet, Macbeth," he threatened. Then he looked down with a comical look of pure outrage. Lugs was peeing into his shoe.

He raised his foot to kick the dog but it scampered under Hamish's desk and lay on his boots.

Blair squelched out.

"Come out of there," said Hamish to the dog. "Do you know something, Lugs? I'm going to keep you after all.

"Merry Christmas, you lovely wee dog. It's turned out the best Christmas yet!"